Be Not Afraid

S·Jean

Also By S. Jean

NOVELS
Hymn of Memory
Born of Scourge
Wherever the Stars Call
Errant Wings

NOVELLAS
Forevermore
The Devil in the Woods

Be Not Afraid

A NOVELLA
BY

S·Jean

CONTENT WARNINGS
violence, gore, references to a sexual assault parallel, electrocution, references to sex, drugs, and alcohol.

For those of us
who can't be pinned down.

Verse One

3AM TIDINGS

Trent was beginning to think he shouldn't have caused problems last week at Geri's Bar. Although, it hadn't been his fault; he stood by that now like he had then. The stool had come at him and he'd done exactly what he should have done and thrown it back. *They* were having a fight. Not him. Granted, the memory of the night was a little soft after that. Maybe more happened. Maybe less. In any case, that didn't mean they had to toss him out on his ass *tonight*.

Barely even had a buzz before some fucker started messing with someone and when Trent cut in, only to get some peace and quiet, the bouncer determined *he* was the cause of the problem and kicked him out! Wouldn't let him back in. He was trouble. End of story. Don't come back.

Fuck that. Maybe they should have remembered further back when Trent's old band used to play gigs there. You know, when they were still friends, still together, still dealing with each other, and he hadn't been excommunicated. Thinking about it pissed him off, so he tried not to. He was a good guitarist, better than the dick they got to replace him. He'd even stayed clean and sober for the last few gigs they did together, but nope. Didn't matter. He was trouble. End of story. Out of the band.

He sighed, trying to center himself. Fuck them. He could find another band. He just hadn't yet, like he hoped they'd take him back if he looked desperate enough.

Which was ridiculous to hope for. Never should have let it enter his mind.

First thing tomorrow: call up Patty. She was always losing guitarists for one reason or another. Maybe she'd have an opening.

But right now, he had to make it to tomorrow morning, and it was cold as balls outside. Middle of winter. Not a penny to his name, already sold his car to make rent (why did rent always seem to go up and his hours go down?), and left his probably empty subway card at home. He was hoofing it. 3AM was not messing around time, not when it was this cold. If he'd known the bar was going to kick him out, he would have already gone home. He'd just wanted a post-work buzz to keep the what-ifs out of his head.

He came up to the park and paused, glancing into it. If he kept following the path around, it'd take another hour to get home. The park was pretty large, like the city was trying to make up for the lack of parks anywhere else nearby. It was nice, if not for it being in the way right now. The city didn't like people cutting through it at night. Something about it being dangerous in the dark, blah, blah, blah. Not that they'd know. It *was* dark, though, almost pitch-black. The streets at least had lights with the occasional cut of headlights from late traffic. But still...

Trent drew his hand into his jacket to catch the guitar pick hanging from its necklace chain. A good luck charm. He'd started carrying it around since he lost more guitar picks than he wanted to admit. At least now, he always had one. He rubbed the face of it with his thumb, across the painted sunflower, and considered the dark.

Ah, to hell with it. Trent grew up around here. He knew how to get through the park without lights. Cutting through was just easier. He shoved his hands into his pockets and forged on in.

During winter, the park was untended. Slush and ice coated the asphalt pathway, making it just a little treacherous. All the benches and other equipment had been pulled into a big storage building to deter loiterers or people chancing sleeping out in the cold. Not that Trent would when it was this cold outside. He could hardly feel his fingers as it was. Home wasn't perfect—a rundown apartment with windows that leaked when it rained—but it wasn't cold.

The path snaked around the park in an undulating line like whoever drew it was drunk, or at least wanted walkers to get a real work out. Not tonight. Trent diverted course into the crunchy snow for a shortcut, a path he'd taken all the time as a teen. Went through the brush, down a hill, and around some trees the city stopped cutting back to hopefully bury the path. It'd take him to a tunnel that cars used to travel across before the city closed it to preserve the sanctity of the park. Now, it was a prime spot to get high and to take cool photos with the band.

It was a more direct path from here to there. Once on the other side, he'd jump a fence and be a few blocks from his apartment. A few blocks from sinking into a warm bed and petting his cat, Scotty.

Honestly, his only friend. At least she still liked him. He was reasonably sure, at any rate. Bribing her with food probably helped.

The tunnel was the same as it had been for years. Grass and weeds grew around it, long and untended, and ivy crawled up and down the walls, taking it over. Sometimes, in the summer, there would be wildflowers. Little blue and white things popping up all over the place. There was a nice photo somewhere of Trent posed with them in his hair as he held his guitar. It was from one of the amateur photoshoots with the band. Probably the best photo anyone would ever get of him.

Now, though, it was a pile of snow Trent

trudged through to get inside. At least here was a reprieve from the wind.

The light deep inside the tunnel had been dead for *years* and the keep-out barriers were cracked. No one heeded their warnings and no one bothered to remove them. Graffiti graced the inside of the walls, artists making a mark for themselves only for their masterpieces to be flaked away and overwritten anew with time.

Trent gave in to temptation and pulled out his phone for a light. He ignored the 5% battery warning (it could never hold a charge anymore), and shined the flashlight on the wall.

"Well," Trent whispered, grimacing. "That sure is a statement."

It was a rendition of Hell. He only guessed it because of the large text proclaiming such along the bottom, the font done in some old gothic look. Figures with horns and bat wings surrounded a bonfire, weapons of all kinds in their hands. Another demon watched over the others from atop his throne of ice—probably the Devil. Fire cut through the image in bold strokes, circling the center and seemed to shimmer as the light hit it. Humans were there too. Tortured. Screaming. Blood and entrails spilled everywhere. The works. At the far edges were angels with white wings staring down at the scene, their forms so pale, they were more like ghosts.

Trent turned his light off and slipped his

phone into his back pocket. Didn't need that to haunt his nightmares. Already had enough of them. He turned away, shoved his hands back into his pockets, and continued on.

His footsteps echoed off the tunnel's concrete walls, making it sound like he wasn't the only one there. Fuck that. He hunched himself tighter and hummed, just to drown it all out.

It wasn't a good song by any means. He hadn't been able to write anything new or good since his band fucked him over, but it was something other than the deafening silence punctured by his own footsteps. Even when it sounded like someone hummed back, he wasn't as unnerved. The echo was playing with him. That was all. Almost comforting.

Just one more block, Trent told himself, licking his lips, and hummed some more. Another verse. This one softer. His fingers itched to follow it with his guitar. Maybe if he'd brought it, he would have felt better.

No, scratch that. He would have gotten mugged for it. Better it was safe at home. He felt for his guitar pick once more, finding solace in it.

One more block. He continued his song and the echo of his hum answered his refrain.

He had some beer at home, at least. Not good beer, but it was something. He'd drink until his head was all fuzzy and distant, and then he'd sleep everything off. Tomorrow, he didn't have work. He could lay in bed all day, never getting out from underneath the blankets. Good plan. He nodded fervently to himself, his hum and its echo trailing off. He'd get through tonight. Tomorrow, maybe. And then...

Then what? What was the fucking point? The question was a thorn in his head. Always there, ready to rip into whatever good plan he might have had. He was a deadbeat. Barely scraping by doing odds and ends for this seedy guy who owned a restaurant across town. Usually, they made him play dishwasher. Except no one ever came into the restaurant. Dishes always piled up anyway. Most nights, he'd get out at 1AM, paid under the table, then he'd do shit like drink himself silly or smoke something questionable until everything was so fuzzy and soft, he could fall right asleep, then he slept. Then it was another day praying he'd made enough for rent. Praying he found another job that paid a little more.

Never did.

Sometimes, his daily life changed. Like when he felt up to playing his guitar, but that was only if the neighbors weren't home. One more noise infraction and he was out on his ass. But it wasn't like it mattered. No band, no reason to play. Patty probably wouldn't need him. She'd just ask his old band why he was a free agent and they'd tell her some lie or another, leaving him as he was. A deadbeat.

Fuck, maybe he was cursed. Life was just one disaster after another. One day, he'd be short on rent. One day, he'd be out on the street with no one to help him. He'd already been ghosted by any friend he'd once had; they'd moved away, made lives for themselves, and he was still here, a deadbeat. The band, what was left of the friends he still had, had decried him as being too much to handle. Family was gone, or at least not worth the heartache it'd be reaching out again. They'd just want him to admit he was a failure and give up his guitar. No chance. Fuck them.

It was just him and his cat.

Scotty. At least he had Scotty. She was always happy to sleep in with him. Happy to meow along whenever he hummed or played the guitar. She kept him going. This was just a rough patch. He'd get through it (right?), and then it'd be okay.

He just wished he believed it.

The tunnel ended. The total darkness melted, letting him out of his thoughts, and he emerged into the abandoned parking lot on the other side. It was clad in somber shades of white and gray from the snow. The blacktop had been iced over, but below, it was crumbling with grass poking up between the cracks. The lone streetlight overlooking this sad patch still worked, its light a soft orange.

Trent wasn't even sure why it was here. It wasn't connected to a road—paved or otherwise.

The streetlight must have been lode bearing; there were a dozen or more wires leading off into the trees. Maybe one day, this light would be gone, once the city remembered it was there. Trent didn't care. He was just glad to see something other than the darkness inside his own head.

That relief lasted up until he sighted five bodies huddled together near the light like they were moths. He stopped dead, his heart in his throat. They weren't there a moment ago.

The bodies didn't move. Their heads were bowed, practically touching one another, as they stared at the ground. If they started singing nursery rhymes, Trent was sprinting away.

When they didn't do anything but stand there, Trent slowly kept moving. Fucking weirdoes in the dark could do whatever they wanted. That could be their streetlight. He'd give them space and go home. Good plan.

Until the light flickered, sheathing the lot in total darkness for a split second. A sudden glitter of crimson caught Trent's attention when the light returned. A vintage Rolls-Royce idled behind the streetlight. Nope. That had *not* been there before the flicker. It was brand new and definitely hadn't braved driving through a park covered in snow.

Trent slowed again, even more confused, and looked closer at the bodies.

One had picked his head up. Scraggly brown hair fell down across his shoulders. His eyes were half-lidded, the shadows making them darker. The others looked the same. They were all wearing brown rags, their bare pale arms and legs sticking out. No gloves, no shoes.

Something was seriously off about this. Trent intended to keep going—fuck whatever weird thing was going on—but then the air shimmered, the phenomena localized around the huddled mass. Like a flame burning through film.

The light above buzzed brighter, flickering in time now with his heartbeat. The huddle looked more sinister as shadows played across their faces. Their expressions were blank, but wrong in a way Trent couldn't put his finger on. What was worse, staring at them spiked a headache through Trent's skull. Like screws were being pushed behind his eyes. Except he didn't trust looking away. You got jumped like that.

Another one picked up his head and turned to look at Trent. Not by turning his body; his neck had twisted itself all the way around, past the point of breaking.

Trent froze. Of course he fucking did. He had to pick his jaw off the goddamned ground.

The light flickered again and then the other four were looking at him.

Their eyelids had peeled back, revealing wide milky-white eyes that glowed. Their mouths slowly split into grins, lips thinned to show mouths of too many teeth.

Trent's pulse raced faster. His thoughts screamed at him to fucking run, but his legs wouldn't. Panic kept him snared right there like a dumbass.

Pupils unfolded in their eyes. Slits at first, running up the brilliant white like a knife cut them through. Then the slits opened, growing wide like a cat's. Their lips quivered and cracked from grins held too long, blood running through their teeth.

Oh fuck, Trent thought uselessly.

Each one cocked their heads. Amused.

Oh fucking fuck.

And that was when dark wings unfurled wide from their backs. One after the other, spreading away from their brown clothes. Loose feathers scattered to the ground, like ash coating the snow.

The first one turned his body to face Trent properly. He folded his hands gently in front of him, like he'd begin praying at any second. His nails were as dark as the night. Skin as pale as the snow around him. His wings were the largest, spreading so wide they could have engulfed everyone inside of them. The light in his eyes grew brighter and brighter, like a bulb about to burst.

"Be not afraid," all five of them crooned.

Verse Two

A CHORUS OF FIVE

"Oh, fuck this shit," Trent hissed.

Before he could do the sensible thing—*run*—the bodies surrounded him. He flinched, a scream dying in his throat, and the wings ruffled wide, blocking his escape. Their bare arms and legs were smeared with ash and grime, skin stretched taut across misshapen muscles and bone to the point to splitting open. Their hands were a mess of broken skin, revealing the sharp bones beneath, blood already dried to black.

"Yes, this one," the first said in a raspy voice dragged up from the depths of his throat. He must have been the leader.

"Yes, this one," the others chorused. A haunting sound, digging itself beneath Trent's skin. He wanted it out of his head. Gone. Not lingering like it did now as a malformed hymnal.

The air shimmered and blurred around the feathers, making Trent's eyes burn. It was then he noticed the neon halo crowning the Leader's head.

A garish white curve, buzzing like a fluorescent light.

Shit, Trent thought to himself. These fucks really thought they were angels. Tripping so bad, they dipped right into delusions of grandeur and plastered a fucking neon light on the back of their leader's head.

Trent threw his hands up. The angels—whatever they were—startled, eyes wide. The Leader was the only one who wasn't shocked; he cocked his head to the side, his smile straining.

"I'm fucking out," Trent said. "It's cold. You guys get home safe too, all right?"

He intended to push through two of the startled ones, but then the Leader's hand snatched his throat. Trent's startled yelp was squeezed silent as the Leader forced Trent to face him again. Blood and decay spilled from the corner of the Leader's lips, a smile held too long.

"Be not afraid; for behold, I bring you good tidings."

Trent threw his arm upward and slammed his elbow into the Leader's face. With a screech, the angel let go, tossing Trent like he was trash. The force of the throw pushed Trent off-balance; he tilted too far to one side, nearly losing his footing, and it gave the other angels an opening. They closed ranks and the flutter of angry wings beat him this way and that. Nails dug through his sleeves, pressing into his skin, and no amount of thrashing threw them off. The angels ignored Trent's cries to be let go and all four tossed him with surprising strength. His back hit the seat of a car with enough force, everything shook.

Gasping, Trent opened his eyes wide. The Rolls-Royce. He was inside it. *The fuck*? That didn't make any sense. He hadn't been that close.

Fuck this! Trent held onto that thought and lunged for the still opened door. An angel coming inside smashed its palm into Trent's face, making him flinch backward to hold his nose. The door slammed shut. Another came in on Trent's other side before he could pivot, and that door slammed too. Two more had slid into the front, their wings spilling around the seats.

The Leader came in last, a shadow made of wings sliding between everything like he was liquid. When he settled on the center console between the front seats, he was solid again. His wings unfurled and revealed his ugly mug again. Despite the bright wash of blood gushing from his nose, he faced Trent like he was a king on a throne.

There were too many wings in one place. Trent could hardly see past them. The two beside him were so close, their feathers scratched against his neck. It didn't help that the angels smelled like fire. Worse, below that, there was something that had rotted from the inside out.

The engine revved and the Rolls-Royce took off, throwing Trent flat against the seat. Knowing where they were—the middle of the goddamn park—Trent expected to hit trees immediately, but no impact came. The Rolls-Royce glided unobstructed, destination unknown.

The Leader watched Trent, pupils narrowed back into slits. His smile grew more and more frightening the longer they held each other's stare. The blood streak from his nose didn't help matters; it made him look even ghastlier.

Trent took a deep breath. "What the fuck do you want from me?" he asked, his voice pitched higher than he'd intended. "If you want money, you've got the wrong guy."

"Be not afraid," the angels crooned. It was hard to tell which one was talking. A dozen different voices echoed across the car, way more than the five kidnapping him, for sure.

Nope. Not happening. Trent threw himself over the one at his side, going for the door handle. He'd rolled out of a moving car before; he could do it again and take an angel with him.

Except, the door handle wasn't there.

The shock hit him so hard, he forgot to thrash as the angel forced him upright, nails digging into his shoulders.

"Be still," the Leader said, annoyance sharpening his voice.

"Why don't you fuck off?" Trent shot back.

The Leader slammed his foot down on the seat. Trent's entire body went cold and he jerked to look. It'd landed between his legs on the seat. Just shy of anything more sensitive. That was a threat if Trent had ever seen one. He swallowed, trying to smooth some of his frayed edges, and met the Leader's gaze again.

"*Fine,*" Trent said, even though it most definitely was not fine. "I'm still. Start talking. What the fuck do you want with me?"

"Must you ask questions?"

"You just kidnapped me. Yeah, I think I'm owed some fucking answers."

A wave of voices conferred with one another, too quickly for Trent to catch any real words. All the angels were watching him, even the ones in the front seat were looking back, completely still. They weren't the ones talking. Trent's nerves itched to escape so bad, but there was no way out.

The Leader sighed, the smile twitching until it had lowered into a scowl. Trent wasn't sure he liked it any better. This looked more like he'd rip out Trent's throat with his teeth.

"Your blood."

Trent blinked. "*What?*"

"Your blood," the Leader repeated like he was talking to a child. The others nodded, repeating his words like they were prayer. "To be fair, any human blood would have done. You are not special before you think you are. Humans always do."

Trent bit down on his tongue. The others chuckled like it was fucking hilarious.

"No human is special. Not even you," the Leader continued. "You are rot. Nothing more than festering rot growing across a perfect world tainted by your touch." More blood spilled out of his mouth as he spoke, sharp teeth grazing the inside of his mouth. "You just happened to see us."

"See us, see us," the others echoed.

"You, your sight, your acknowledgment of our existence in your world pulled us fully through. But truly, any mortal blood, any mortal eyes would have done. So long as your blood is warm to the taste, life singing through each drop, it will wake God."

"God?" Trent repeated.

"And since you were there," the Leader went on like Trent hadn't even spoken, "and you saw us, your blood is ours for the taking."

Trent brought up his foot and kicked the Leader as hard as he could. The angel snarled and shoved Trent against the seat, holding him there with a clawed hand. In an instant, he was mere inches from Trent's face, baring rows of sharp, misaligned teeth. Trent stared at him, unwavering, and dared the fucking angel to do something.

The angel didn't. Glared furiously, sure, but that was it. Trent almost laughed.

"This is bullshit," Trent whispered.

"Can't we take his blood now?" the one to Trent's right asked, shaking him.

"Yes, yes," the one to Trent's left said, nodding.

"Let's take it now."

The Leader jerked his glare toward them, head twisting around like a bird's. The two flinched, like they were struck. "Do human hearts beat after extraction?"

Extraction. Trent was definitely dead at the end of this ride. So, so fucking dead. His skin went so cold, he felt faint. They really were going to kill him. He needed out, stat.

"No," one angel said, almost unsure of itself. Trent couldn't tell which one had spoken.

"No," the Leader agreed, his head twitching to stare at Trent again. His pupils unfolded wide again. "He must remain alive and whole until the appointed place."

The car dipped, like it was heading down an incline. Trent held himself to the seat and looked wildly at the windows. Where the hell were they? The city was fucking flat, no hills to be found until at least an hour's drive out. All he could see past the rustle of feathers was a pitch-black.

The road became steeper and Trent struggled to stay seated. The angels didn't move, like gravity wasn't affecting them.

Trent tried to breathe evenly. This was fine. Just a normal, steep as fuck hill with freaks. Eventually, they'd have to stop and he'd run.

Breathing evenly lasted until he saw fire streaking by the windows. Heat seared through the air, making it warble. But just as quickly as the heat arrived, it was stolen away with a frigid blast snaking itself inside of Trent's clothes. All he could think of was that damned mural. All the painted blood and torture. Shit. Had it been a warning?

The Leader laughed, a low staccato that didn't really sound like laughter. It echoed from somewhere beyond him, filling the car like everyone else was laughing too. They weren't. They were just smiling wickedly. The Leader snatched Trent's face suddenly and forced Trent to look at him. His halo was even brighter now, burning its afterimage into Trent's vision.

"It'll be over soon," the Leader crooned as the car leveled with a thump. "You won't even know. God will wake. All will be well. As above, so below."

"As above, so below," the others echoed.

As if waiting for the cue, something solid smashed into the hood of the Rolls-Royce. It hit with such force, the back end went up, leaving Trent and the two angels in the air for a brief moment. When the car landed, the angel in front was turning the wheel so hard, it sent the car spinning. The inside descended into pure chaos. Voices shouted at one another, ordering each other on what to do. Feathers ruffled as arms shot out to help the one in front steer straight. The Leader was screeching for everyone to listen, but no one was.

Trent took advantage of the chaos; he smashed one angel in the stomach with his elbow, making it double over. He chucked the other at the

Leader, making the angel cry with surprise. The car finally stopped, the brakes squealing, and Trent jerked forward. He lurched away from the mess of feathers and limbs as quick as he could, but before he could smash a window and get out, everything stopped. Stilled. The angels looked upward, like they expected some sort of divine intervention. Trent couldn't help himself and did too.

The softest touched landed on the roof of the Rolls-Royce.

It was another held moment before a crunch of metal pulled the roof aside like the car was no more than a can. A figure loomed atop the car, one with glowing blonde wings. That was all Trent saw before a lead pipe came down. It smashed into the Leader's head, cracking through his halo, and caved his head in. Blood went flying. He shrieked bloody murder, flailing useless arms, and as another angel tried to grab the assailant, the lead pipe came down again, pulverizing the outstretched arm.

Trent didn't need to see any more to know this was his chance. As the blonde wings went ham on the angels, lead pipe flying up and down, spraying blood all over the place, Trent threw himself out of the car.

He landed hard on ice-cold asphalt and picked his head up. An angel screeched and grabbed his legs, but as he turned to kick them off, the lead pipe broke through both of the angel's arms. Another spray of blood doused Trent's would-be savior. A pair of glowing eyes, glittering bright with too many colors to name, met Trent's. Except fuck if he was going to trust them. Those were *wings*. Fuck trusting angels.

His kidnappers dragged the new angel down, screaming louder as they tried tearing into them and Trent took advantage of the distraction and escaped.

Everything was dark. The horizon a pitch-black omnipresence. A red glow rimmed it, outlining vague shapes in the distance, giving everything a sinister crimson shade. As he swung his gaze this way and that, he saw a real light. A gas station with bright lights above its pumps.

Deserted, but better than here. There had to be someone inside. Trent forced himself forward, ignoring how stiff the cold made his legs.

The pumps were turned off, looked not quite right with details just shy of being realistic, like someone had drawn them from memory, but Trent didn't want to linger outside. He went for the glass doors. When they didn't open at his approach, he cursed and cupped his hands together to peer inside, hoping to flag someone down. What he saw didn't fill him with confidence; there was *nothing* but empty shelves. Cobwebs stretched from one corner to another, everything was covered in a thick layer of dust, and no one was inside. That couldn't be right.

"Shit," he breathed and spun around, flattening his back to the glass doors.

Everything had gone eerily silent. He couldn't even see the car anymore. He darted his gaze across the dark and his heart sped faster. Sitting here would get him kidnapped. Or beaten with a lead pipe.

He took off his jacket and wrapped it around his fist before he smashed his hand through the glass door. He'd expected it to take a few punches, but it caved in so easily, like it wasn't at all what it seemed. None of this was; Trent stopped caring.

Once he had enough clearance to reach the lock, he undid it and shoved the door open. There had to be somewhere inside to hide and get his head on straight to fucking think. Or maybe fucking wake up. That would be better. He threw his now glass-ridden jacket aside and hurried inside.

The front was too open with useless empty shelves he couldn't hide behind. He swerved to the counter and peered around to the back. The Employee's Only bathroom. Good enough. He slid across the counter and clattered into the back.

Besides the bathroom door, there was nothing else but piles of trash and outlines of what must have been there before. Eerie, but didn't matter; Trent wasn't here to loot the place. He slammed into the bathroom and shut the door. There was no lock—of course there wasn't—and he cursed.

The lights flicked on at his intrusion, making him flinch, and when he opened his eyes again, he bit back a yelp.

Every wall had been marked with words. *Help. Help me out of here!* Blood was pooled around the toilet. A box cutter was on the floor, the blade rusted with gore.

"Shit, shit, shit," Trent breathed, his voice a squeak of panic.

Another light flicked on. He startled, throwing himself at the opposing wall. It was just the mirror above the sink. Except, it wasn't his reflection. Someone else stood there, staring inside, with a whole different bathroom behind them. This one looked like what one would expect from a gas station bathroom. A little graffiti, but no repeated cries for help.

The person peering into the mirror was dressed in a simple polo with the gas station's logo on the front. A worker. Trent threw himself at the sink, waving, but the worker didn't look at Trent. They were fixing their hair.

"H-Hey!" Trent shouted. The worker didn't acknowledge it. They'd bent their head low to wash their hands.

"Hey!" Trent screamed louder, pounding on the mirror, but it did no good.

It was like Trent wasn't even there. The worker finished and left. The lights on the other side went off, leaving the mirror a dark reflection of Trent's own panicked face.

Adrenaline was wearing off. Trent was shaking. Breathing ragged bursts of panic. He didn't know what to do. How he even got here. How to even get home. What—

Glass crunched outside from a soft step.

Swearing again, Trent threw his gaze over the room, searching for a weapon. Box cutter was too small. He needed something with longer reach. There was a mop tucked in the dark corner. Good enough. He grabbed it, positioned himself in front of the door, and waited. No lead pipe was going to take him by surprise. He'd get out and pick another direction to run. There *had* to be a way out of this nightmare.

The steps were silent now, too soft to hear beyond the pulse thumping in Trent's ears. Trent held his breath, waiting. And waited some more.

The doorknob turned. Trent tensed. The door opened inward and Trent went out swinging.

The angel with the blonde wings dodged to the side, the dirty mop head missing them by mere inches. "Be not—"

Trent twisted and swung again. The pole slammed into the angel's stomach, making them double over with a strained gasp, and Trent threw the whole thing at them to run. Wasn't gonna give the angel a chance to grab him, no fucking way.

As he sprinted outside, he remembered how

dark it was and loudly cursed. Thankfully, some of the darkness had parted; the Rolls-Royce was on fire now, a large flickering flame in the middle of an empty lot. The top was peeled back, the windows were busted in, and the angels lay bent and broken around it, their wings and limbs a mess of blood, snapped bones, and feathers.

Good riddance. Until one of the wings twitched. Until an arm more bone than skin shoved itself upward from the heap. Then another and another. Wings rustled, feathers falling off in heaps only to be replaced by new ones.

The angels were still alive, even after all that.

Glowing eyes from the mass of fluttering wings opened and settled on Trent. Anger surged off the stare as the pupils violently twitched back and forth. Trent's heart leapt back into his throat.

"Oh," he breathed, "hell fucking no."

He picked a direction, prayed, and ran.

Verse Three

GLITTERING EYES

When Trent lost sight of the gas station and the smoldering wreck of the Rolls-Royce—the darkness folded over them when he was far enough away—he found another street. An empty six lane main road, crumbling with potholes and fissures. The sound of cars penetrated the air, but nothing was physically there. Just more darkness.

Buildings flanked the road on either side, but each one was shut tight. Barbed-wire wrapped around door handles, large shutters blocked entrances altogether, and most of the time, they were obstructed by piles of trash or rusted fences. A few windows high out of reach were lit up neon red, looking far more sinister than they had any right to be. No one was peering out, but Trent expected to see bright, bloodshot eyes watching him every time he glanced upward.

Farther down the road, past all the inaccessible buildings, Trent came up to a motel. It stood out like the gas station had, lights so bright in its windows, Trent couldn't see inside. More importantly, it was a beacon. Another place to hide with many rooms inside where he could figure everything out.

The automatic doors slid open as Trent neared them, letting him inside. Potentially a good sign. The lobby was deserted aside from the front desk. A lone CRT monitor from a bygone era emitted scanlines, lighting up the wall behind it. The walls were cracked, the wallpaper warped from dilapidation and singed from a past fire. After debating about hiding under the desk and resolving he wouldn't fit, Trent hurried down the carpeted hallway. There had to be an open room. One preferably with a lock.

Before he'd reached the first room, the motel shook. The automatic doors chimed, but then glass crunched, like they were forced open. Trent whipped around. The ceiling lights were flicking off and on, and in between beats of darkness, a halo raged bright. Newly reforged from broken glass, it scraped across the ceiling as a body floated inside.

This wasn't the five angels from before. This was something else.

Five pairs of ragged wings folded across a shadowed body within. Deep pools of black eyes peeked out from beneath the feathers, rimmed in light that lit the face set crookedly to one side. Arms hung loose at its sides, bones sticking out of the skin, leaving rivulets of red running down the limbs. Its legs were the same, the blood slipping down into the floor around its bare feet.

The hands came together in the front, gently clasped. The eyes stayed wide inside their ruffle of feathers, never breaking away from Trent's.

"Be not afraid," it chorused, the voice a legion of many.

The overhead light flickered off and then on. The horror was closer. Each time the lights flickered, it had moved, leaving behind ashened footprints in its wake.

Trent hauled ass in the other direction, trying every door he could reach, and the lights only flickered faster, compounding his panic. The chorus of *be not afraid* came closer, filling the hallway, only broken by the beats of light and dark.

A door finally pushed inward beneath Trent's frantic scrambling. Just as he allowed himself a relieved breath, a hand came out of it and took him by the front collar. A pale, dainty hand. Not an angel's with broken skin.

It tightened around Trent's shirt and threw him into the room. He fell onto his back, losing his breath. Before he could get up, the door slammed shut, and a body came down on his, straddling his waist to pin him there. A hand flattened against his mouth, smothering the scream in Trent's throat. He wanted to thrash, get up, but then he noticed it was the blonde-winged angel on top of him. The one that had helped him. Twice now.

A willowy body of soft angles. Cheeks dusted with white freckles like stars below dried blood. Brilliant, glittering eyes of so many colors, like a prism. They had fluffy white hair kept short, much better maintained than the five angels from before. Across their bare shoulders were detailed wing tattoos, the feathers reaching down past their biceps. Their black tank top and shorts were soaked with blood, but their bright red high tops somehow escaped the earlier carnage.

The angel outstretched their free hand toward the closed door. With a deep inhale, words cascaded like song from their lips, verses Trent couldn't catch. The air shimmered, a softness descending on the room in response, and soon, the door glowed. White lines crisscrossed into the grain, swirling into symbols Trent didn't know. Looked like it was out of some occult playbook. It must have been real, though. The way the song settled inside Trent as he listened felt warm. Maybe not the occult, then. Maybe something divine. The warmth maneuvered itself between Trent's muscle and bone, creating a home there as it did in the door.

The song tapered off, as did the warmth, and the angel met Trent's gaze so directly, he flinched. They put a finger to their lips, like they feared Trent would start screaming any second.

Maybe that fear was warranted. Trent had half a mind to throw the angel off his lap—how much could they weigh, really?—but stopped himself. He was safe here, as awkward as it was, and instead, he listened to the scratching in the hallway.

Something sniffed on the other side of the door. Another thing crooned sadly. Nails raked across the wall, trying to find purchase. The horror darkened the space between the door and the floor, blocking out the hallway lights. An acrid taste coasted through the air the longer the horror stayed there, like ash and blood. Trent held his breath.

"Where did he go?"

"He was just here!"

"Why did that one interfere?"

"We will kill him!"

"We told you we should have brought the human fast food..."

"WHERE DID HE GO?!"

The final question was a chorus of a dozen different voices, loud enough to shake the door. Trent startled, but the hand on his mouth smothered any shout of surprise. The horror hesitated on the other side another moment before the voices began arguing with each other again. The shadow went away, the voices becoming quieter and quieter as it moved on.

Only when it was gone did this angel of blonde-wings remove their hand.

Trent threw the angel off, catching them by

surprise, and scrambled to get away. His back found the wall near the bathroom entryway and he used it to brace himself into a sitting position. The bathroom light turned on, sensing him nearby, and it lit the angel in a soft, gauzy orange. There was a coy smile on the angel's lips as they began to speak. Trent cut them off.

"You say '*be not afraid*' one more time, I am going to fucking freak out."

The angel blinked and shut their mouth. Now that Trent wasn't panicking and now that there was ample light, the angel was actually kinda cute. Blood notwithstanding. Trent slapped his face with both hands. Not the time to be taken by a pretty face.

The sting of the slap helped him reorient his thoughts. He glanced at the room past the entryway. Barebones. A single bed, no blankets. An old TV spewed static. There was a window left open at the far end of the room, letting air smelling of fire and frost blow inside. Must have been how the angel got inside.

The bed caught Trent's attention; it was *moving*, the bedsprings squeaking rhythmically. Trent blinked, staring at it, and the angel looked too, leaning forward to see. They snorted. Trent glared at them, confused.

"Why's the bed moving?" Trent asked.

The angel tilted their head, amused. "Our worlds are... mirrors of each other," they said. Their voice was easy to listen to. Soft. "Therefore, this room exists on your end, too. Sometimes, strong feelings and corresponding motions can manifest here."

"Ah," Trent said, calming down a fraction from an actual answer, as weird as it was. He stared at the bed another moment and bit back a laugh. "So, there's probably someone fucking on that bed, huh?"

The angel hummed. "Likely."

Trent looked at his savior again. The angel sat there, knees up to their chest, patient. The lead pipe lay across their lap, speckled with blood. A little concerning, but Trent couldn't find it in him to be afraid. There was something familiar there in the angel's eyes, like Trent had seen them before. Even the smile. The soft way their eyes crinkled with the motion. Except Trent couldn't place it. Not right now when half his thoughts were still scattered by panic.

"I'm Trent," he introduced, figuring he had to start somewhere. "He's good if you need it."

The angel nodded. "That's good for me too."

Trent waited and when no name came, he cleared his throat. "Uh, what's your name?"

"Oh." There was a soft disappointment in the angel's face before he shook his head. "I don't have one."

"Did those five have one?"

The angel shrugged. "Of a kind, but we are

different."

"I gotta call you something," Trent said. "Do you want a name?"

As the angel thought about it, lips pursed in thought, Trent let himself calm down just a little more. This banality was helping. It was also, unfortunately, letting him realize how exhausted he felt from all the running.

When the angel still didn't answer, Trent thought of something and forged on just to keep himself distracted from the aches in his legs.

"You look like this guy I met once," he explained, piecing the images together in his head. Same haircut; fluffy and short with an undercut in the back. The guy's had been more strawberry blonde, though, not this shocking white. Still...

"His name was Seth."

"Seth?" the angel tested the name, rolling it across his tongue curiously.

"He came to see my band play at this New Year's gig last year at this grungy basement bar," Trent explained. It was a shit gig, honestly. Barely got paid. But that Seth had made it worth it. The way his eyes glittered seeing them up on the stage had done something to Trent's heart. Everyone else had been so absorbed in themselves, only Seth had really listened. Gave Trent goosebumps whenever he thought back on it. Something about those eyes.

"After the gig, I danced with Seth while

another band played. You look like him. Cute guy."

Trent wished he'd left off the "cute guy" bit as soon as he'd said it. Especially when the angel looked absolutely delighted, his wings perking behind him.

"Yes, I accept it. Hello, I am Seth. It is a pleasure to meet you, Trent."

The clinical way in which he agreed made Trent laugh. It came out a little unhinged, but sorely needed. A spill of nerves once bubbled up, now escaped with the sound. Seth laughed too, his voice a little softer and more confused than anything else. Trent got a hold of himself before long and wiped his cheeks.

"Sorry. Just... This is a lot," he admitted. He swallowed another bout of stress-induced laughter and nodded. His insides still felt like they wanted to fray apart from nerves. "This... This is all real, isn't it? Not some fucked up nightmare where I'm really passed out in a ditch?"

Seth's smile dropped. "It's real."

Just what an unreal angel *would* say. Trent accepted him at face value anyway. There was enough pain across his body to say it probably wasn't a dream.

"Shit." He scrubbed his hands down his face and sagged against the wall. "Okay, okay. What the *fuck* is going on? You saved me. Twice."

"I did," Seth said.

"Why?"

Seth shrugged.

"Are you like them?"

"Sort of." Seth glanced over his shoulder and his wings twitched. They were definitely more translucent and much smaller than the previous five's wings had been. Each feather was overlaid on top of the next one, making it not seem as translucent as it was.

"Those were... Seraphs," Seth continued, sounding unsure of the name himself. "I am barely an angel. A maybe-angel is typically what I'm called. These wings are sewn on. I wouldn't normally have wings nor the power of the divine magic that comes with them."

Too many questions to ask there. Trent took it at face value again. "Okay, and you're not working for them?"

"No."

Needed more than that. "Start from the beginning or I am crawling out that window and taking my chances in the dark."

Seth's face scrunched, annoyed. "You won't get far."

"Try me."

They sat there, glaring at each other. Trent didn't know what was so hard about answers, but he was tired of waiting for them. When he made to get up, Seth jerked forward to his knees and put out his hands, worried.

"Stop, I'll explain more."

Trent gave him another moment of silence. When no explanation came, he huffed. "Well?" he asked and Seth sat back, tucking his legs underneath him. "Come on. I think I'm owed an explanation."

With a long sigh, Seth turned away. He must have been searching for the words. How hard was the truth? When Seth found an answer, he looked back at Trent, determined. He moved much more fluidly than the five from earlier. Hell of a lot realer, too. Maybe he really wasn't with them.

"As I said: those were seraphs. A higher tier of angel," he explained.

"So angels are real?"

"... Yes," Seth said slowly, "of a kind. They may not match what you're used to, but that is the closest term to which I can describe them for you to understand."

"I'm not religious," Trent said and Seth exhaled, like a weight was taken off his shoulders. "They got feathered wings, I guess that tracks. If angels are real, are demons?"

Seth shrugged. "Of a kind. You'll mostly find them in call centers trying to make deals to get your soul."

Yet another reason to ignore any and all unknown calls. Trent nodded. "What about that *thing* that almost got me? What was that?"

"Also a seraph. Technically, its true form," Seth explained. "They are five, but also one. That thing is all their minds working in tandem to achieve the same goal. They tend to default to it when they are wounded beyond divine repair."

Snorting back a laugh, Trent nodded with a barely concealed grin. "You got them real good with that pipe," he said. Seth smiled shyly at the compliment, dancing his delicate fingers across the pipe. "Any other angels to worry about?"

Seth gave it some thought, tilting his head. "If pushed, seraphs will call in an archangel. Those are made for battle and there's no lead piping my way to victory with them."

"Why not?"

"A lead pipe will not withstand a flaming sword."

Trent shuddered. "Noted."

"Other than them, nothing of true note. Angels who watch from the skies don't tend to come down. There are also cherubs who watch gates that will never open again, but they don't fight..." Seth paused, thinking. "And many more that don't deal with a seraph's machinations. We just need to worry about the seraphs."

Good to know, Trent supposed. "What do they want with me?"

"To wake God."

Stupid question. The five freaks had said the same thing. Trent dragged a hand through his hair, wishing he had a cigarette so his hands had something to do. "What does that do?"

"It resets the world," Seth said and hesitated

when Trent gave him a look. "You and all will cease to exist."

"What?"

"Your blood will bring about God's awakening. It will allow the seraphs and archangels and every being in their pantheon to once more be in the Grace of God."

That didn't help make sense of shit. Trent huffed, frustrated. "And how does my blood do that? The freaks said it sings with life?"

Seth was looking frustrated too. "You are alive in ways we are not. Your blood sings with the Word of God, what He pushed into humankind when He set the wheel in motion. Its return means things are out of alignment. It will wake Him."

There was a pause.

"Supposedly," Seth added, rather coyly.

Trent raised an eyebrow. "Supposedly?"

Seth shrugged. "Well, they haven't actually done it yet, have they?"

Point taken. If they ever had, Trent wouldn't be here. He rolled his eyes. "All right, sure. Makes enough sense." Didn't. Not really, but he was rolling with it. Trent still wasn't convinced this was wholly real—this all sounded like dream logic—but it wasn't like he knew what else to do but believe. "And you?" he asked. "What's your skin in the game? Why save me at all?"

"You're cute."

The comment fried something in Trent's

brain, he was sure. He sputtered on his words and gave himself a moment to catch up. No way. That wasn't what Seth had said. "Excuse me?" Out of Trent's throat came a dry laugh. "You think I'm cute?"

Seth narrowed his eyes, confused. "You do not believe me?"

"Fuck no," Trent said. He scratched at the patchy stubble lining his jaw. His hair must have been a mess, too. Not to mention all the blood splattered on him. "No way. Try again."

Sighing, Seth sagged his shoulders. "Fine," he said. He met Trent's gaze again like a challenge fully accepted. "I want to crack you open. Eat your bones. Pull you apart to see your heart. Feel you on the inside. Feel what it is to have you inside me the same." Seth paused. "Is that acceptable?"

The room became silent. Save for the bed still creaking away. Trent cleared his throat.

"Can we go back to me being cute?"

Seth had the gall to look triumphant. His wings twitched. Trent took that to mean he was happy. "Thought so."

Angels were fucking weird. Didn't match up to anything Trent had ever heard, but to be fair, that was rather small. Trent also hadn't liked what Seth's clinical description had done to his heart. The little happy flip it'd done when half of it sounded outright horrifying.

"Is that really it?" he asked.

Another sigh left Seth's lips. "I like the human world," he admitted softly, like it was a bad thing. "I'd hate to see it all gone by the whims of the seraphs. Although..." He frowned, glancing away. "I guess I'd be gone too, so I wouldn't even know. If they have their way, there's no need of me either."

Self-preservation was a reason Trent could get behind. Made a lot more sense. He nodded, like he actually understood it all (he didn't), and hated (and liked) the way the agreement made Seth's face brighten.

"All that from my blood, huh?"

"Supposedly," Seth repeated. "They are incredibly bad at handling humans, however." He drummed his white nails on the pipe. The click-clack was in time with the infernal bed. "The human dies because the seraphs forget how fragile you are. That's more inevitable than them winning. Chances are, they would have accidentally killed you before you even got near God."

"And you think I'm cute enough to intervene and risk saving?"

"It would have been a waste," Seth said. "I thought I could help."

Trent was alive, at least. That was one point for sticking with Seth beyond stroking his own ego. "We just need a way out then," he said. "A way to get me home. Got a plan?"

"I'm thinking."

They went silent, save for the bed. Trent glanced around him and grabbed some crumpled newspaper that had been piled near the bathroom. Text on it was illegible, like someone only had a rudimentary idea of how text looked. He tossed it at the noise. It hit nothing. Seth snorted back a laugh, biting his lip. Trent grinned at him.

"That's pretty distracting, huh?"

"It's very distracting," Seth agreed.

"They're *really* enthusiastic."

"Too enthusiastic. I'm worried their hearts will give out before long."

That got a real laugh out of Trent and he was glad Seth joined in, his wings twitching more. Some sense of normalcy bloomed between them, putting Trent more at ease.

When their voices trailed off, Seth cleared his throat. "While I've never sent someone home," he admitted, "I do know we need to go somewhere the walls between our worlds is thin."

"Those seraphs took me here in a fucking Rolls-Royce."

"Yes, but that is outside my powers."

"If I go home, will they kidnap me again?"

Seth shrugged. "Don't stare next time. That's what allows them physically into your world for a brief moment."

One more fuck up to add to the list and a new thing to be paranoid about. Trent thumped his head against the wall. It echoed into the bathroom and he grimaced. "You sure this place isn't thin enough? Even with our honeymooners over there?"

"No," Seth said. "I think—"

The door shook, heavy fists pounding on it, and both of them jumped. Seth shot to his feet, eyes wide, and Trent came up too, holding his breath. The pound came again, rattling the entire doorway like it was about to come down. The white lines and symbols melted away, leaving blackened roots crawling through the door. Trent's heart picked up speed.

"The fuck?" he hissed.

"They've found us."

Verse Four

With one more pound, the door hinges came loose. They plinked uselessly to the floor and the door began tilting inward.

Seth grabbed Trent's shirt and hauled him into the bathroom alcove. Another horror show waited them inside. Tub blackened with rot and blood. Sink stained with red. Rust at the edge of everything. The worst of it? No weapons.

The door blew inward with such force, it ricocheted off the walls and into the room. The fuck-bed kept right on creaking, none the wiser. The bathroom light above them fuzzed off and on, little sparks spilling out of the bulb from the horror's intrusion. Even the lamps in the room did the same. A frenzied panic at what was coming.

And slowly it came. The horror glided inside, feet barely touching the ground while the longest of the feathers dragged on the floor behind it. The halo was eye-searingly bright, shining a light on the grotesque skin peeking out from beneath the feathers, its bulging eyes flicking this way and that. It smelled like death and fire this close, almost making Trent gag.

Seth braced himself, taking the lead pipe with both hands, and as the horror passed the bathroom alcove, he charged. A hand of too many fingers snapped out of the feathers and snatched the pipe out of the air. The seraph hadn't even *looked*. When it finally did, it was as a twitch of movement between lights sparking, its neck turning all the way around. Bright eyes flashed and the arm lifted the pipe higher, leaving Seth's legs dangling.

The eyes looked past Seth and caught Trent. The pupils flared wide, almost absorbing the light inside the irises. A hymn of reverberating screams erupted from the seraph and pushed itself through the room. Trent hunched over in pain, covering his ears. The hymn dragged itself louder and louder, digging itself underneath his skin, until the seraph cut it off to slam Seth into the opposite wall. The maybe-angel hit it hard enough, the wall cracked beneath his back. Seth gasped, eyes fluttering wide, and slumped to his knees on the floor.

The seraph turned and took up the bathroom doorway. Trent had nowhere to go. No weapon to defend himself. The seraph reached forward with a hand of split fingernails and broken bones, but it didn't touch Trent. The lead pipe came swinging through the ruffle of feathers. The weight of it took off the entire arm. Blood sprayed all over the bathroom, coating everything.

"Run!" Seth shouted, an ordered hymn carried upon the word. Warmth curled through Trent's legs, giving him strength. Seth dodged a swipe coming for his head, ducking low, and the seraph fully turned back to the angel, screaming with a million voices.

Trent dove out of the bathroom, shoving himself below the flutter of feathers. When he hit the opposite wall, he rebounded off it and stood. Seth let out a pained grunt and Trent turned, half a step to the door.

The seraph had cracked the pipe in two. Seth let it go, but another arm jutted out from the feathers and snatched him up by the wing.

And ripped.

Seth arched his back, gasping. His blood splattered across the seraph's feathers and the walls. When the seraph let him go, all he could do was slump to the floor, prone for another attack. Trent wouldn't let that happen; he dove for Seth's wrist, intent to drag him away, but Seth was just as fast to recover and throw himself at Trent. They clattered out into the hall, Seth stronger than Trent expected. As Trent got his bearings, Seth rolled them both to the side, dodging the seraph's next attack. The floor where they'd been crumpled like wet paper from the foot stomp, but that was all Trent could see of it before Seth was at his feet and dragging Trent after him.

"I said: RUN!" Seth shouted.

As the seraph behind them shoved itself out of the room, the windows in the lobby crashed inward. A mass of seraphs, identical to the five that had kidnapped Trent, were trying to get in. Their arms reached inside, hands grasping at nothing, and broken glass cut through their skin like it was tissue. Too many eyes peered inside, spotlights tracking everything. The discordant hymn of *"be not afraid"* rumbled out of the mass, shaking the whole motel.

Seth pushed Trent into the far wall, dodging a large hand swiping their way. A string of curses made its way out of Trent's throat as he reoriented, trying to think of a plan. Seth wasted no more time thinking; he dragged Trent further into the motel, a plan of his own clearly forming.

The hallway twisted, this way and that, lights turning off and on in a panic. The horror was screaming. More seraphs clattered inside, bare feet and hands slapping against the ground as they took chase. The whole hallway shook, tripping Trent up, but Seth kept pace.

A neon exit light hung over a set of back doors in front of them. Trent almost slowed to take a breath, but Seth jerked him to a skinny hall he wouldn't have seen on his own. His shoulders barely fit inside, but Seth shoved him farther in.

"There! Down there!" Seth ordered, pointing.

"This is a way I come and go here—just get down there, *now*!"

A fucking hole with a ladder like you'd find in a pool was at the end of the hall. Except the rungs were rusted through. No way it was going to hold Trent's weight. He didn't have time to deliberate. The lights turned off and stayed off. He threw a panicked look over his shoulder. The halo was there in the dark, lighting up the seraph's twisted face. Eyes opened up wide, rings of garish light searching for them. The body tried to force itself inside this crevasse of a hallway, but it was too big.

Fuck. No.

As fast as he could, Trent flew down the ladder. The rusted rungs cracked beneath his weight, and the entire thing shook as he scrambled downward. As soon as he touched the floor below, Seth slid all the way down.

Once beside Trent, Seth led them forward.

The hallway looked like it shouldn't have existed, like it was a crack carved through what was normal. Sure, there were walls, but they were haphazardly put together with plywood planks nailed together and beyond them was a rusted fence. The floor was a steel grating with only darkness below. The only light they had were red emergency lights strung from plywood post to plywood post, wires tacked to them with staples. It didn't feel real.

"There's an elevator at the end," Seth said, out

of breath. Trent picked his gaze up and saw it: an industrial elevator with a metal gate, all the way at the end, wreathed in red lights. "It goes to the subway. Just get there and—"

He stopped, eyes wide, and looked up. The ceiling bowed above them, just shy of cracking. Seth shoved Trent just as it gave way. The horror came down, all feathers and wings, and pinned Seth beneath its large hands. Trent scrambled back to his feet, ready to throw fists, but Seth had it handled. He slammed his palm upward with such force at the seraph's head, when it caught, the horror's neck cracked. A cry of pain echoed out of the mass, shaking the hall, but it wasn't dead. The hands slammed Seth's head back into the floor.

As the horror pulled Seth back up to do it again, the maybe-angel turned his brilliantly bright eyes on Trent.

"Go! *Please!*"

Not without him. Heart ramming against his ribcage, Trent threw himself into the fray. Just like a bar brawl, only with feathers instead of limbs. He ducked underneath the flailing wings, and threw a punch as hard as he could. It collided with something solid, soft, and another scream erupted. It let go of Seth for a moment and Trent took the chance to drag the angel out from underneath it.

Seth spared Trent a soft smile, the expression making Trent's own lips twitch to follow the motion, before they sprinted for the elevator. Seth threw the gate open, pushed Trent on, and slammed his fist against the basement button. It lit up.

They were safe.

Until hands jutted out of the darkness beneath the horror's feathers. Trent saw them coming over Seth's head and grabbed Seth. It wasn't enough. All the hands had to do was tug once and Seth jerked out of Trent's grasp. Seth flew backwards, dragged by his remaining wing, and was slammed against the wall. Trent fell back the other direction, banging against the back of the elevator. The entire thing jostled and the gate came down, sealing him inside.

"Shit! No!" Trent surged upward and tried to shove the gate aside, but it was stuck tight.

Seth screamed. Trent froze and looked.

The seraph had torn off Seth's other wing and threw it. The delicate bones cracked as it hit the elevator fencing. Seth lay face down on the floor now, arms shaking as he tried to get up, but the seraph came down on him before he could. A hand dug into his head, grinding his face into the floor.

Shit, he couldn't fight back like that. Trent pulled at the gate harder, trying to get out, but it wouldn't move.

Feathers cascaded over Seth, covering his body almost completely like a shroud. Everything was dark inside. A growing darkness becoming solid. It oozed over Seth's legs, holding them still, and more hands came, digging fingers into Seth to stop his struggling. The seraph dragged Seth's head back by his hair and all Seth could do was shake his head, eyes wide with panic.

"Come on!" Trent shook the elevator gate as hard as he could to dislodge it. It had to open. Seth needed his help. "Please!"

The elevator chimed almost mockingly and gave way then, plummeting downward. Trent fell, hard, unable to stay standing.

"No, no, no!" Trent forced himself back to his feet, his skin cold with panic. "Stop! *Please!*"

The elevator didn't listen. All Trent heard beyond the squeal of gears was Seth's anguished scream. But then it died. Replaced with a guttural growl ripping through the air, the sound tearing Seth's voice in two.

Shaking too hard to stay standing, Trent collapsed to the floor. No, this couldn't be happening. He'd just left Seth there. Like a coward. He could have fought harder. Done more. Not let his hand go, for fuck's sake. Trent's breaths came out as a wheeze. His cheeks were damp with tears. He'd just left Seth there. He repeated it to himself, mouthing the words over and over again, as they sank in. The one person willing to save Trent and he hadn't been able to do the same.

When the elevator came to a stop, it did so abruptly. The whole thing jerked violently and the sudden movement sent Trent vomiting in the corner, unable to hold it in anymore. Acrid beer and bile came up. When it was over, all was still. Silent. More tears slid down his cheeks and he shook his head.

"Shit," he heaved, his stomach trying to expel everything he had in him, "shit, shit, *shit*!"

Nothing responded. Not even his own echo.

Verse Five

SINGING STRINGS

The elevator gate fell outward, crashing to the ground, and Trent jumped. He whipped around, squeezing his fingers into fists, ready to go out swinging, but nothing was there. An emergency light blazed uninterrupted further down. Industrial pipes lined the ceiling, radiating heat, and the walls were made of gray cinderblock. Even the floor was a solid slab of concrete. It was like a different world, but Trent doubted it was his own.

Swallowing all his fear and regret, Trent crawled out of the elevator. No one was there. Just him and the silence screaming in his head.

Trent forced himself upward, using the elevator as a crutch to make sure his legs could hold him. They could.

The elevator didn't respond to him slamming the buttons to go back up. Nothing was lit up anymore, well and truly broken. He was stranded. He swore, slamming the control panel as hard as he could with his palm. Didn't help. Just hurt his hand. Frustration bubbled below the surface and he dragged his hands through his hair.

The scream Seth had made reverberated through Trent's skull still and he squeezed his eyes shut, sick again. Fuck, none of this was right. It was all wrong. Angels didn't exist. Towering monstrosities called seraphs didn't exist. This whole world didn't exist.

Except it *did*. Trent couldn't will it away. Every breath meant it was real. All the aches and pains, and the taste of bile in his mouth, too. He opened his eyes. Nothing was going to wake him from this nightmare.

A sound echoing toward him made him flinch. He flattened against the wall, holding his breath to listen, but it was just a subway rattling somewhere beyond the walls. Seth had said to go for the subway. Had to be a way out, then. With a deep breath, Trent listened to his maybe-angel.

Still, he was scared shitless, jumping at the shadows he made as he stalked down the hall. It was cold, the heat from the pipes useless against the chill. He regretted losing his jacket. Even glass-ridden, it would have helped. A short-sleeved band shirt wasn't doing enough.

Desperate for more light, Trent patted down his pockets until he found his phone. Screen was beyond cracked, but he figured it would be after all that. He tried the side buttons, but the screen stayed dark. There was no indication that his phone was even alive.

Sighing deeply, Trent paused to gather himself. He was shivering. From the cold and shock, probably. Both mixed together in a hideous feeling festering in his gut. The frustration of everything was so close to boiling over, but he had to keep it together. If the seraphs caught up to him, he needed some clarity of mind so he stood a fighting chance. He slid his phone away and took the guitar pick from beneath his shirt. He rubbed his thumb over it, gathering a little solace. Once he was sure he wasn't going to break down, he tucked it back into his shirt and continued on.

The hall took him down a short flight of stairs adorned with caution lines on each step. At the first landing, a small hallway jutted off toward a row of glass doors. Beyond them was pitch-black. Trent watched the dark for longer than he should have, waiting to see something but his own tired reflection, but nothing was there. He didn't trust it. Not with how many seraphs had descended on the motel. They might have been waiting outside.

He continued down the steps until they opened up at the bottom. Lights shined brighter here, thankfully, and revealed a subway platform. The tail end of a subway trundled by on the far side, the taste of steel coating the air in its wake. Comforting, reminding Trent how much he used to sit on subway platforms with his guitar when he was younger.

One side of the platform had a large route map, but it was so distressed and old, Trent couldn't even begin to read it. The other side had a graffitied entryway to a pair of bathrooms. Pillars decorated in caution lines went up the middle of the platform, the advertisements tacked to them too garbled to understand. Words were mashed together to look just real enough, but it was like whatever made this world didn't understand what made one word different from the next. There was a busker, too, at least, the sound of one. A violin specifically, but Trent couldn't see them. Must have been another mirror into the real world.

The sound gave Trent a little more comfort. An actual noise so he wasn't stuck inside the screeching silence of his own head. His fingers itched to follow the melody and he wished he had his guitar.

Numbly, his feet took him to one of the pillars to lean against it, but his legs had other ideas. They folded underneath him, hoping for a reprieve. No reason not to give them one; he slid down until he was sitting and pressed his back to the pillar.

"Shit," he breathed, letting everything settle even though he didn't want it to. All he wanted to do was keep ignoring everything that had just happened, if only to maintain his sanity. His chest was heaving suddenly, his lungs starved, and it felt like nothing would go in. He pulled his knees close and ducked his head between them, lacing his fingers behind his head. All the earlier panic came back in a new wave. One threatening to crush him underneath it.

This was fucked. Well-beyond fucked. Trent slapped the back of his head, willing himself to wake up. This had to be a nightmare. Tears trickled out of his eyes despite him trying to squeeze them back.

Trent was going to die. The seraphs would find him and he'd die. That would be it. What a shit life, too. He'd burned every conceivable bridge these past few years, no one was left to miss him.

Well, his cat would. Shit. What if no one checked on Scotty? She was orange. No brain cells. Only cat. She'd starve without him. She didn't deserve that.

He couldn't just sit here and wait for his demise. For her sake, at least. It was something small in the grand scheme of things, but he held onto that and let it give him strength.

Another subway flew by, shaking the place, and Trent squeezed himself tighter.

"Okay, okay," Trent said, trying to psyche himself up. Coins clinked against an unseen violin case near him. The song grew softer with a new tune, and it pressed into Trent like a friendly touch. "I'll get out of this. I gotta do it for her. I just gotta figure out *how*. Fuck! Fuck, fuck, fuck!" With each fuck, Trent raised his voice.

He should have done more. Shouldn't have left Seth. But then what would he have done? Not gone through the park at fucking 3AM, that was for sure. They'd both be alive, then. Wholly unaware of one another and would have moved on with their lives. Maybe if Trent hadn't talked—fucking flirted—so long in the goddamned motel room, they could have gotten out before the seraphs came in. Trent gripped his head with both hands, pressing himself even tighter, like it would help his racing thoughts settle. Help the panic attack bubbling under the surface soften.

A hand smoothed over his knee.

The sound from his throat wasn't one he was proud of. He jerked his head upward and fell sideways trying to get away. On his way down, he saw familiar glittering eyes. The white hair. The light, stardust freckles. And Seth's fucking coy smile.

"Shit!" Trent shouted, panic shoved back into high gear as he forced himself upright.

Seth held up the offending hand. "Do not be—"

"Don't you dare tell me not to be afraid!" Trent spat out, his voice shaking between panicked decibels.

With a tilt to his head, Seth put his hand on his knees. "Okay," he said. "I won't."

They sat like that, Trent flat against the pillar and Seth crouched in front of him, staring at one another as the violin kept singing. Seth didn't *look* dead. Harried, maybe. Trent swallowed and took stock of what had happened to the maybe-angel.

Dried blood pocked the skin across his face around the scabs up near his hairline. Nails had raked across his neck, leaving bright, angry welts. It even went down to his shoulder, the cuts drawing across the wing tattoos like it'd wanted to claw them off. His tank top was in shreds, barely holding onto one shoulder and the bottom had holes ripped into it. Shorts were scuffed and torn as well. Long angry welts continued across his stomach and his hips, bright against his skin. The rest of him was still intact, just a bit more blood-splattered and bruised.

Most importantly: alive.

"You're not dead," Trent said, more of an affirmation for himself than anything else. "I thought that thing killed you."

With a roll of his eyes, Seth stood. The motion made him wince, but he was quick to hide the expression. "You're being dramatic. It can't kill me. Not in the way you're thinking." He gazed around the platform and stopped, hopeful, upon seeing the graffiti-laced bathroom doors.

Trent scrambled to his feet, holding onto the pillar behind him in case his legs had other ideas. "All that blood?"

Seth shrugged, peering up at him. "They tore off my wings. It's to be expected." He pointed at the bathrooms. "If you don't mind, I'd *really* like to wash some of the blood off." He glanced down at his shirt, grimacing, and picked at it. "And change..." He didn't wait for Trent's reply before heading over.

"Ch-Change?" Trent trailed after Seth, trying not to look at the angel's exposed shoulder blades, where the wings had been. Wasn't pretty. It made Trent's stomach sick.

"I have a little stash here for myself and others," Seth explained. "With any luck, it won't have been raided."

Compared to before, the angel's voice was short and clipped. It put Trent on edge, like Seth blamed him that all this happened.

"Hey, hold on." Trent picked up the pace when Seth showed no intentions of stopping. "Seth. Seth, wait. Just hang on a second. Talk to me." He stopped the maybe-angel with a gentle hand.

Seth's entire body flinched and he spun to face Trent, slapping the hand away.

"Don't touch me," he snapped, his voice sharp. "And stop saying that name like that."

Trent hesitated, feeling the heat of Seth's glare. It was like he'd combust beneath it. He nodded mutely and held up his hands. "I'm sorry. I just... I want to make sure you're okay."

Seth watched him, his gaze intense, before it softened with an exhale. He crossed his arms and held himself tightly. "It's nothing to really talk about. It happens. It's what I'm for. It... It leaves me out of sorts."

There was some nuance there Trent was missing. He waited, hoping for more so he knew how to help, and Seth made a dramatic sigh.

"Look, I can explain and clean up. I just really, really want to wash off the blood."

The lights buzzed on as they entered the bathroom, soft orange fluorescents hanging from the ceiling. A reprieve from all the bright whites. There were a few stalls riddled with graffiti, a lone sink still standing amongst the broken ones, and a mirror across the wall. It reflected them, helpfully, and not a dark void. Despite the graffiti and the state of literally everything else in this world, the bathroom looked acceptably clean. A relief.

Seth passed the sinks and a few stalls before he opened the one at the very end. Trent remained near the door, giving the maybe-angel some space.

It still felt like Trent had to say something. "I'm sorry," he tried again. "I didn't mean to spook you before. I was just worried."

"I know," Seth said softly and reached inside the stall. He came out shortly with a bundle of washcloths, a bottle of soap, packages of gauze, and a roll of medical tape. He returned and spread it out across the sink.

"But I'm a maybe-angel, remember?" Seth said, like it explained everything.

"I still don't know exactly what that is," Trent reminded with a crooked smile.

"We're not real. We're just fodder for the seraphs to use and discard."

The water from the sink came out crystal clear. Seth let it run until steam wafted upward. Carefully and deliberately, like he'd done it so many times before, he began washing up the blood. Trent stayed uselessly to the side, ready to help if needed, although he had no idea how.

"You see," Seth continued, watching Trent through the mirror, "seraphs don't know what it is to be alive and nor can they hold form in your world for very long by virtue of the world not being made for them. They found a loophole. Made things like me. Maybe-angels. We watch the human world, we listen to your radio stations, watch your shows, whatever. We absorb what you are, make sense of it, and the seraphs take those experiences from us so they feel alive. Sometimes, when we become more formed like I am, they're able to let us out into your world to gather *real* experiences. The truth of them."

"Experiences?" Trent asked.

Seth ducked his head and pressed the slowly-turning-red cloth to his face. Water dripped down, clearing the blood and grime from him with little effort. "Life, I guess. I'll have about a day to go out and do something. Go to a bar, listen to a band, check out a museum. Sometimes, I go to this cat café I really like. In any case, it's just some experience where I feel truly alive in some small or large way. At midnight, or thereabouts, I'm pulled back into this world where... where..." He hesitated, tapping his fingers on the sink. Sighing, he dipped his entire head under the faucet, letting the water run through his hair.

When he came back up, wiping his hair back, he found the words. "They eat me."

Trent couldn't help but shudder, eyes darting back to the angry marks all over Seth. Bite marks. Those were definitely bite marks of jagged teeth dragged across flesh. Not nails. All he could think of was the terror in Seth's eyes when the seraph had him. The scream he'd made before it was cut off entirely.

"Shit," Trent whispered.

"Apt word," Seth agreed. "But sometimes that's not enough. Sometimes, they have to... Push themselves into the core of my being just so they can have something to take out of me if I'm resistant. Taking it scrapes the experience from my insides so they can feel it exactly as I did." Seth pulled off his shirt and left it on the floor. When he pressed the washcloth to his sides where more red marks were, he hissed in pain. "That's probably the worst. I can still feel them inside of me sometimes."

Oh, Trent thought to himself. He paused, watching Seth again. He had a strong desire to hug the maybe-angel, but jerked his arms back to his sides. "I'm—I'm so sorry."

"There was nothing you could have done." Seth opened a package of gauze. It was then Trent noticed how bloody Seth's knuckles were. "We like the experiences that make us feel real, so it's always like that when we come back. We don't want to give it up. Seraphs force it out of us. It's all we're here for, after all, according to them."

Which explained why the seraphs were so angry Seth had intervened at all. He wasn't supposed to be anything more than what they'd made him for. Instead, he was wielding a lead pipe and beating the shit out of them. The earlier beatdown must have been cathartic.

Trent gently edged closer and took one of Seth's hands. Seth let him have the gauze too.

"Is it always like that?" Trent asked, gently wrapping the gauze around the knuckles.

Seth shrugged, watching Trent work. "I've known it no other way. Usually, I lose every bit of who I am, all of it stolen and absorbed by them. I'm reduced to not even having a body. I'll reform sometime later, a new body, a new me, empty memories with broad strokes of who I used to be."

When Trent finished wrapping his knuckles, Seth flexed his fingers. They moved fine and he gave Trent his other hand. This one had fared better, but the wrist didn't. Gouges cut across the inside, peeling away the skin. Trent got to work wrapping it up gently.

"Except," Seth continued, the ghost of a defiant smile coming to his lips, "that doesn't actually happen anymore. They can't take any experience from me any longer. What's mine stays with me, no matter how many times they try. It pisses them off, though. Makes what they do worse because I remember it more vividly, but I get to keep who I am."

Trent hesitated and glanced at Seth, worried.

"I must have seen or done something too human for them to process and it stitched itself into the core of me. Making me real."

Seth had said it all so distantly and quietly, Trent wondered if it had been his choice. Seth wouldn't look up at him; he kept his eyes on the sink, on the rush of water steaming the mirror.

"When they're done and high off whatever they think they scraped," Seth continued, "the seraphs are easy to escape. Just lay there and endure it all until I see an opening. They'll be mad when they realize how starved they still are." A dry laugh came from Seth's lips.

"Are you sure you're okay?" Trent asked.

Something about the question made Seth pause. He blinked a few times, like he was pushing back tears, and finally smiled up at Trent. There was only sadness in it, though. Not the teasing coyness Trent had become accustomed to.

"Do you know they never let us see dawn?" Seth whispered. "When we're on your side? It's always less than a day."

Trent paused. "Really?"

"Yeah. Is it pretty?"

The change of topic was so obvious, but Trent accepted it anyway, nodding. He didn't have to drag an answer out of Seth. Whether the maybe-angel was truly okay or not didn't matter; Seth had to keep moving. Dwelling wouldn't help anything. Trent left the topic alone and fully accepted this new one.

"I think it is," Trent answered. "Especially when it all lights up pink and orange." He gently nudged Seth. "Maybe you can see it one day."

Seth looked away, shaking his head. "Maybe. Can you help me with my back? It's okay if it's too much, though. But it'll speed this up."

A physical way to help. Trent took it because he desperately wanted to help.

Gingerly, afraid to hurt Seth, Trent began cleaning out the gouges the torn wings had left behind. Seth kept himself braced on the sink, biting his lip. The wounds weren't as large as Trent had first guessed. Most of the blood must have come from the wings. To distract himself as he gently wiped up the blood, Trent traced the feather tattoos with his eyes. Each feather had been immaculately done, the detail exquisite. They sloped down Seth's arms and went across his shoulder blades where the gouges were. Maybe they were from an experience, although Trent wondered just how long ago they'd been inked and how they'd stayed. Maybe a question for another time.

Trent took another cloth from the pile Seth had brought, leaving the bloodied one in the sink, and gently washed away more gore. He was mindful whenever Seth hunched himself tighter, his head ducked in pain, but the maybe-angel urged him to continue each time.

Once Seth's back was cleaned and dried, Trent began applying the gauze and tape.

"Are you going to miss the wings?" Trent asked, wanting something other than silence.

"Not really," Seth whispered. "I stole them from another angel. I'll miss the divine magic they gave me more than anything else."

"Divine magic?"

"Every being here has access to it, it's just about how much." Seth watched Trent continue working through the mirror. "Different wings give me different powers. Those were from a regular angel and I purely used them for their energy and strength. Nothing really important."

"Did you kill the angel?"

Seth smiled wickedly, making Trent shiver. "They started it. I have my own divine magic without them, though all I can do is heal wounds. Doesn't work on me. Just other maybes."

Trent secured the pieces of gauze and added a little more tape for good measure. Once he was done, Seth tested slowly rolling his shoulders. Everything held.

"You should clean up too," Seth said. "You look like hell."

A laugh bubbled out of Trent's throat. The audacity of this guy. "Pot calling the kettle black, there," Trent teased.

Trent was glad Seth giggled, even though he turned his head to hide his smile.

It didn't take Trent as long to wash up. The warm water felt heavenly on his face and arms. Scrubbing the blood away made him feel more human, like he really could go home again. Gave him a little more hope, at least. When he finished, leaving his shirt the way it was because there was no saving it, Seth nodded appraisingly.

"Much better," he teased. "Now, let me find new clothes."

Seth went back to his stall and Trent followed this time, silently hoping there was something for him in there too.

The stall was more of a cramped pantry. The toilet wasn't even there. A wooden pallet was instead, keeping a nest of blankets and pillows off the floor, and shelves surrounded it on all sides. One was full of items that looked like they'd been pilfered from a pharmacy. The other set of shelves had clothes of all kinds piled together, towels and washcloths, and even an old radio. Seth extended the antenna and turned it on. It picked up a soft jazz station and the notes soon began playing off the walls and ceiling.

Better than silence. The acoustics here weren't even that bad.

"Did you lug all this from the human world?" Trent asked.

"Some of it was me, yes," Seth replied and dug out a sealed water bottle from the pharmacy side. He handed it over and Trent finally realized how thirsty he was.

Trent chugged it down. Cold as ice, but refreshing in all the ways that mattered. When he was done, he wiped his mouth with the back of his hand.

"Could we trick them to sending you on an excursion? Smuggle me out?"

"Not after the number we've done on them," Seth admitted as he returned to the shelves. He began digging through the clothes. "Besides, even if we hadn't, I don't think I could smuggle a whole human. They'd notice. You don't exactly fit in my pocket."

First that came out of the pile of clothes was another band shirt. Too large for Seth and he held it out to Trent, hopeful. Trent didn't recognize the band, but it looked real enough. A pair of bright white eyes with a sword between them was the logo. Trent traded his shirt for this one, happy to have something clean.

"I like your tattoos," Seth said after Trent had

changed. "The sheet music on your sides is nice."

Heat crept to Trent's cheeks. He hadn't realized Seth was watching him. "Just the first song I made on my own," Trent said, suddenly shy. It wasn't even that good of a song now. "Wish I had money for more," he said. "Thanks, though."

Seth resumed digging through the clothes. "Does it hurt to get a tattoo?"

Trent snorted. "You have wings tattooed on your shoulders."

Seth hesitated, glancing at them. "I don't remember when I got these done," he said. "That experience is gone. I'm surprised they've lasted this long. My body's reformed at least a few times since then, I'm sure."

"Oh." Trent felt like an asshole. He cleared his throat. "It really depends on where you get the tattoo done. Somewhere fleshy is better. Did you want another one?"

"Maybe," Seth said and turned his attention back to the clothes. "Flowers would be nice."

"They'd look nice on you," Trent said. "Maybe cherry blossoms?"

The shy smile Seth tried to hide made Trent happy. "Maybe," Seth said.

Seth found a tank top buried somewhere in the center and tugged it free. He measured it to himself before he yanked off the store tags. Not from anywhere Trent knew. Seth threw it over his arm and went digging for more, having to stand on his tip toes to reach the higher shelves.

"So, is all this just from excursions?" Trent asked, still wanting something other than silence and the soft jazz. He gazed over the pharmacy side, wondering how Seth smuggled it all by himself. Surely not one trip.

"Not always," Seth replied. "Sometimes, items just appear in this world. Like... When something mysteriously goes missing on your side? Chances are, it found a thin spot and simply rolled through."

Trent snorted, nodding. "I've lost a lot of guitar picks like that."

Seth smiled at him over his shoulder. "Is that why there's one hanging from a chain on your neck?"

"What if it is?" Trent teased and pulled at the chain. "I won't lose it this way, right?"

With a knowing nod, Seth went back to moving the clothes, searching for more. "But yes, whenever I, or another maybe, finds something that isn't trash, we put it in caches like this. Sometimes, demons will tease seraphs and throw things into this world. Sometimes, it's literal trash, but a lot of the time, it's helpful for us maybes. I think they feel bad for us."

"You think?" Trent asked.

Seth shrugged. "There's a demon I meet sometimes. He thinks I'm cute. He'll steal me stuff I ask for whenever he's out hunting souls."

"Can he come here?" Trent asked.

"Not for long. The air burns his lungs since he's definitely not meant to be here. I usually only see him if we're both in your world briefly. A shame, really." Seth found what he was looking for and held it up to the light to inspect it. A pair of shorts. Not new, a little distressed around the pockets, but in way better shape than his shorts now. A new pair of socks came out too.

Nodding to himself like he was pleased, Seth kicked off his shoes and bent down, pulling his ruined shorts with him.

Trent quickly turned away, flustered. Could have given Trent some warning before he undressed. He bit back from saying so, and waited while Seth got changed.

"You mentioned demons work in call centers before," Trent said.

"Yep, I did," Seth agreed. He paused and made an annoyed sigh. "Well, *those* don't fit..." He grumbled to himself and resumed rustling through the clothes. Trent continued looking away.

"How does that even work?"

"They find a mark and leave their card. You call the number and one hooks you for your soul. It's all rather methodical. Demons don't even like it, but I suppose it gets results." Seth spoke so nonchalantly, like it was a regular, no-nonsense thing. "I tricked my demon for an experience that way. He was mad when he realized I had no soul to give, but we're friends now."

"You don't have a soul?"

Seth hummed and Trent listened as he tried on another pair of shorts. "Souls are the core of humanity. I'm not human," he explained. "I don't know the details or even what having a soul means. I suppose they're important if demons want them and humans don't want to lose them."

"What do demons do with souls?"

"I'm actually not sure. I don't usually talk jobs with my demon. Seems like it'd be rude."

"What *do* you do with your demon, then?"

"Casual sex mostly," Seth replied. "But I'm sure you don't want to hear about that."

Trent scrubbed a hand down his face. "Yeah, I think I'm good."

The ensuing silence left Trent attempting to process everything. It was still too much. First seraphs, then angels, then maybe-angels, and now demons and souls. All of it hidden right next to his own world. So close to everything he knew, but also not. He ran his hand through his hair, pushing it back. Nothing made sense. He had so many questions, but he doubted he'd get real answers for them. He tried one anyway.

"So... Is any religion even right?"

"I wouldn't know," Seth said from beside Trent. He was smiling again, all dressed. A white tank top with a deer printed on the front hugged snugly to his torso and he'd paired it with a pair of black shorts with high contrast stitching. Socks were fresh and white again, no longer the blood splattered tatters. "Aw, did you care about my modesty? I wouldn't have minded."

Trent pushed him, flustered, and Seth giggled. Artfully dodged the question, too, but Trent let it go. Not all questions had answers.

"Those seraphs will continue coming after you. Probably with an archangel in tow soon," Seth went on, back to business.

"Great."

"Summoning one takes time, at least."

"How can you tell they're summoning one?"

"Vibrations. I can feel it. The hymnal they use is echoing softly against the air."

While Trent couldn't feel anything of the sort, he took Seth's word for it; he was only human, after all.

When Trent made no follow-up question, Seth reached back into the pantry stall. The soft jazz music faded, the last lingering echoes of it growing silent. When Seth came back out, he'd pulled on a white and red satin bomber jacket. There were embroidered flowers along the black sleeves, cherry blossoms, making Trent smile.

"We have to get gone before the archangel arrives or we're not escaping," Seth explained.

Sensible. Trent nodded and Seth held out something else for him. Another jacket. The black denim paled in comparison to the leather one he'd had, but the gesture was touching. Trent took it and looked it over.

The outside was a little worn and rough, but it had a soft plaid lining on the inside that almost looked new. Patches decorated the back and front. Most of them cool, like the devil wings on the back. The eyeballs on the sleeves. Trent dug the whole vibe. He threw it on, happy to see that it fit.

"Thanks," Trent said and Seth smiled brightly at him. The maybe-angel handed him a few more bottles of water, too, which fit snugly inside the jacket's interior pockets.

"All right," Trent said, as prepared as he was going to get, "where are we gonna get gone at?"

Seth folded his arms in thought, but didn't answer right away. He silently led them out of the restroom and back to the unseen violin player. Someone had joined in with a sax. The two instruments sung into the tunnel, notes echoing off the subway tiles, and Trent couldn't help but tap his foot to the song.

After a few moments of listening, Seth gasped and faced Trent, eyes bright.

"Ah, I have an idea!" he said, excited. "Places of worship tend to be the thinnest between our worlds. Easy to cut open and stitch back together."

"You've done it before?" Trent asked.

Seth made an uneasy motion with his hand. "No... But the theory is sound. There's a church at the end of the line here. We take the subway, get there, find a way inside where there is holy water, I do a little divine magic, and bam. You're back home." He waited a moment as Trent considered it, before he drew closer, hopeful. "I've never done it before, so I cannot promise you with any assurance that it'll work, but it's all I have. Is that acceptable?"

The question was asked so softly, like Trent would say no. He watched the maybe-angel. Seth was smiling again, like he had before the seraph had gotten him. Like nothing had happened.

Burying something as horrific as that so quickly without giving it time to breathe bothered Trent. It was going to fester. Trent couldn't keep the concern to himself and his mouth was moving before he thought better about it.

"How are you fine?" he whispered and Seth's smile faded. "I really, really thought you were dead because I wasn't fast enough. A-And then knowing what it was doing?"

Confused, Seth tilted his head. "You were really worried about me?"

"*Yes*," Trent breathed. "I don't want you to get hurt helping me. I don't deserve it."

The shyest smile graced Seth's lips. For a moment, he glanced everywhere else before finally resting on Trent's gaze again. He gently reached up and adjusted the collar of Trent's new coat. He smoothed out the lapels and patted them. "See," he said, sounding a little embarrassed, "you're cute."

The words rang familiar in Trent's head this time. He'd been called cute plenty of times, even if it really wasn't really true, but it was the soft way in which Seth said so. The tenor of his voice suddenly familiar. Even the motion of adjusting his collar.

A shiver went down Trent's spine as he studied Seth again. The brilliance of his eyes caught his attention. The familiarity in them that Trent couldn't put his finger on before, but now, the way they sparkled beneath the lights? It was like the Seth from his memory.

Had the same glitter been born of the supernatural back then? Trent had figured it was the rows of lights the bar had across their ceiling. But the eyes were the same. This Seth was thinner, smaller, but he was moving just like the other one. Same motions. Same shy voice. It couldn't have been a coincidence. Especially now that Trent knew maybe-angels came into his world, searching for experiences. Could it have been this Seth?

The possible realization knotted itself on Trent's tongue. Why hadn't Seth said anything if that was true? Was it an experience stolen away like Seth's tattoos? Trent wanted to ask, to be sure, but stopped himself. Would it just remind Seth of all the experiences seraphs stole from him? He'd sounded so sad not remembering the origin of his tattoos. Trent didn't want to make him sadder. Yet the burning desire to ask won out. Trent opened his mouth, deciding to hell with it, but then the subway arrived.

The screeching brakes drowned out the sax and violin and the entire thing came to a shuddering halt in front of them. Seth turned away, facing the subway, and Trent swallowed the question. No more distractions. Getting out alive was more important than answers.

The subway cars were a grimy silver, the logo along the side incomprehensible as it merged with the many different names the subway must have had throughout time. Each window was bright from the lights blazing inside and it almost hurt to look at it.

"Here's our ride," Seth said softly.

Verse Six

ESCAPE ROUTE

The subway doors hissed open, pushing a cloud of warmth into the platform, and its entrance stole Trent's question away. He shook his head. Not like it mattered. If—*when*—he survived, then he'd consider asking again. Assuming Seth somehow managed to come through with him. Trent hoped he did.

Though Trent made to step onto the subway, Seth put out an arm to stop him. Shadows bubbled at the doors, some formless thing, and then bled out. Trent jumped behind Seth, who was wholly unconcerned. Seth *waved* at the shadows, too, a bright smile on his lips. Trent thought it would end there, until the shadows made an appendage to wave back.

"What are those?" Trent hissed, scrunching himself tighter to hide behind Seth.

"Those are more maybes. What we start as before our bodies take shape," Seth explained as the shadows passed around them like a current.

Seth gave a few more a cute wave, whispering a soft hello, before returning his attention to Trent. "Chances are, they are walking in step with a human on the other side, waiting to have a chance to go out there. If you act human enough, form a body that almost *looks* human, seraphs take note and send you."

Trent squinted, trying to see the humans the maybes were clearly following. Nothing. Just a wave of shadows. "Can you see the other side?"

"It's... It's in shades. It's hard to explain." Seth drew a hand over his face and gazed toward the violin and sax player. "I can see them play, the motions their fingers are making across their instruments, but nothing more concrete than that. It's something with our eyes. If these maybes get bodies to go out there with, they'll have eyes that look like mine."

A mess of brilliant glitter. Some maybes already had eyes like Seth's, little glances here and there peering out of the shadows. They were just as quickly folded back into the dark.

The shadows continued passing them, the chatter of a subway platform coming to life for the morning rush in their wake. The violin and sax continued their routine, louder and playful now, and more coins clinked against instrument cases.

"Are the seraphs going to eat them too?" Trent asked.

The smile faded. "Eventually," Seth whispered.

"All we are to them are experiences to be devoured. Our essences are vomited up eventually and thus, the cycle continues. I hope they all survive."

Trent glanced at Seth, hearing the sadness in his voice. "It's shit," he said.

"I know." Seth nodded, sighing the words, and turned away. "But what can we do about it? Seraphs rule this world by design. We're their tools so they can pretend this world is like yours, a world that was never theirs to begin with."

The last trickle of shadows exited the train, chattering happily in echoes Trent couldn't understand.

"Why can't it be theirs?"

"God made humans and gifted them the world," Seth explained. "You are a manifestation of His word, His love. Seraphs had a role at some point, but their time has long since ended. They linger now, decaying all the while. They fear dying, so they do this on the chance it'll save them, even if it means returning humanity to a null existence." Seth tugged on Trent's sleeve and nodded toward the subway. "Come on, let's get on before it leaves."

The inside of the subway car was pretty standard. It was grimy, had a weird odor like the subway Trent was used to, and had the same triangle patterns on the cushioned seats. Graffiti riddled the walls, words here and there like there had been a conversation once upon a time. Trent couldn't follow it. As he tried to decipher it anyway,

Seth went to study the glowing map near the opposing door. Trent gave up on the graffiti and looked over the map too.

Similar to the routes back home, but these lines crisscrossed haphazardly with no rhyme or reason once they left their stations. Trent could barely begin to follow it, but Seth had no problem. He pointed at the end of one line.

"We're down here and this route goes up like this," Seth said. "Is it different than your side?"

Trent gave him a tired look. "This looks like gibberish to me," he said. "I don't think seraphs know how to make a world."

Chuckling, Seth nodded. "Seraphs don't have an eye for detail beyond cars, so I am not surprised it's wrong." Seth continued to draw his finger along the path, all the way up to the end at the Elmwood Road Station. Trent knew that station, at least. There were a bunch of different little establishments right outside it and definitely a church he'd never set foot into.

"If we stay on this line, we'll end up here. I know of a place of worship there."

Unease itched under Trent's skin as he mentally mapped the street in his head. "We won't get out right at the church if it's like back home," he said. "Unless you have another way in like the motel..."

"I do not."

"Then won't they see us?"

"Yes…" Seth drew out the word, voice tight, and considered the map again. Walking there from another stop didn't seem smart; they'd be out in the open for too long. Besides, who knew how many dead ends there were out there.

"We'll have to run. Can you?" Seth asked.

Trent snorted and smiled wryly. "I guess if I have to," he said. "What do we do when we get to the church? You said something about holy water?"

The subway chimed a destination, interrupting them. The voice was metallic and sounded like it spoke backwards. Seth headed to the seats and sat just as the train began its glide forward. It wasn't smooth. A rock to-and-fro that Trent was expecting. He caught himself from leaning too far with it, wanting to get lost in something he actually knew, and instead, sat next to Seth. Normally, back home, the cars were too packed to sit anywhere, especially when he used them. Sitting was nice, even if the seats left a lot to the imagination. The view kind of sucked, too; it turned pitch black after leaving the station, the only lights coming from the tunnel too erratic to matter.

"I can use the divine power in the holy water to carve a hole into the world," Seth continued finally. "All you'll have to do is jump in. We'll have to be quick, though. Places of worship are where angels gather to try and feel real from snatches of prayer." Seth leaned back, stretching his legs to cross them at the ankles. "They'll probably get me, but as long as you get out..."

Nausea licked up Trent's throat. He swallowed it and tried to scrub the memory of the seraph out of his head. "You don't gotta do this," he whispered. "This putting yourself in danger just for me." When Seth didn't look at him, Trent forged on. "I mean it. Why do you want to do this if it'll end like that?" He wanted an honest answer this time. Seth regarded him curiously. "Not just 'cause I'm cute. Not just to save my world. You said they'll probably kill me before they even get me where they need me. That's easier, right?"

Even if it'd be sadder.

Seth cut his gaze away. "Yes, there is a certain self-preservation to saving you. If the world goes, so do I. Although, you're right. It *would* be easier to be rid of you right now." The words sent a chill down Trent's spine, but Seth was smiling softly. "But it'd be a waste."

"I'm not anyone special," Trent argued, not sure why beyond his desire to dig for more of the truth. "I'm barely even *good*. Seriously. I drink too much. I get into fights over the stupidest shit. I can barely hold down a job. I'm not worth this. I'm not important enough to put yourself through hell."

"Who cares if you're important or not?" Seth asked simply and Trent was stunned silent. "I live in a world where decaying seraphs decide what is important. They put themselves at the top, everything else below them to be used and discarded.

They are *not* more important than you or me." Seth's voice was becoming more and more incensed as he spoke. "Maybe I want to show them how useless they are by saving you from right under their noses. I want to fuck with their plans to prove I *can*. That *anyone* can. They deserve to know just how badly they've failed."

"Ah," Trent said. Screwing someone over just to prove something, Trent could get behind that. He couldn't even hide his grin.

"I'm sorry you are being used for this," Seth added hastily, and looked shyly at him.

"No, no, it's fine." Trent waved his hand, snickering. "That was well-spoken. Middle finger might have been easier, though."

Seth returned the grin and nudged Trent with his knee. "Besides, you being cute is a perfectly fine and valid reason, regardless if you're good or important. Those qualities don't matter to me. I don't have to choose anything grand as my reason. Little things matter, like seeing you alive."

Hearing so touched Trent deeper than he thought it would. After everything with the band, just knowing that someone liked seeing him alive, was sweet. Way kinder than he deserved, maybe, but Trent tried ignoring that part.

Maybe Seth was right. Grand things didn't matter. They didn't happen very often, anyway. Life was made up of the smaller things. The very things Trent looked past in a life coming apart.

Maybe it still sucked, but there were things he could look forward to. Like his cat, another gig maybe, playing his guitar for the stars, and even seeing Seth again one day.

Absolved, at least a little bit, Trent leaned back and rested his shoulder against Seth's.

"Why do you think I'm cute so bad, though?" Trent asked. He had to know. "This place is leaving me pretty scruffy, not gonna lie."

Seth happily leaned against him, staring up at the lights. He closed his eyes, like he was reliving a pleasant memory within them. "When you hold the guitar, when you play it... It's... It's sublime. I couldn't stop staring. I can't let the image go. You were so vivid and right. Like you were plucking the strings of me. I never felt that before. Maybe I just think that you're cute for that alone. It could have been anyone, but that night, it was *you*."

Trent stopped, his heart fluttering. No. Screw waiting to ask if this Seth was really the one he'd once met. This had to be important; that explanation cemented it. He glanced at Seth and whispered, "when did you see me with my guitar?"

The answer never came; anything Seth had gone to say was stolen away when the subway jolted violently, like something landed on it from above.

Verse Seven

HAIRLINE FRACTURE

"No, no, no!" Seth flew to his feet, eyes wide. "How did it find us so fast?"

The lights flickered off and on. Trent's stomach sank, his heart gearing back up into panic. An eye peeked in through the glass skylight above, its ring of light wreathed in rustling feathers. Its gaze darted this way and that, until it landed on Trent and Seth. It twitched faster, enraged, becoming a blur. Fists came down on the roof, shaking the entire car. Seth snatched Trent's wrist just as the glass cracked, and dragged him into the next subway car.

Glass crunched in the first car. Trent swung a look over his shoulder; the skylight was in pieces on the floor. A screech came down, its weight making the subway cars buckle as it landed. The subway lights burst then, one by one up and down the cars, and Trent pulled Seth close to cover him from the falling glass.

In the dark, wings ruffled. Lights from the

subway tunnel outside cut across the inside, illuminating the horror in snatches. Scattered feathers resembled ash, coating the floor. Broken limbs forced the horror to its feet. The single eye between the wings was large and bulbous, its iris bright. Other eyes grew inside of it, pushing each other out of the way to fully open.

Every single eye landed on Trent and Seth. The horror stood so still, Trent wondered if time had stopped.

Glass floated up from the floor, molding itself into a neon halo. The broken shards fixed to the back of the seraph's head, buzzing on. It was so brilliant and bright, it made Trent flinch to hide his eyes. Once his vision cleared, he regretted looking back at the horror.

What was once sort of recognizable as a torso, arms, and legs, had become a bundle of limbs folded over one another again and again beneath the feathers. A pair of arms hung limp at the sides, another folded across the chest a dozen times, while the last pair brought its hands together in front.

A cut of light dragged across the seraph and then it was closer. Again and again, just like the flickering lights. Anything in its way was crushed and thrown aside, like the subway was paper beneath the seraph's presence. Windows cracked, standing poles came down, seats warped. Total destruction.

Seth had sense; he gripped Trent's wrist again and together, they ran. No matter how fast they went, however, the horror and destruction quickly gained on them.

They reached the last car before long. No way out. A dead end. Seth swore and turned on his heel. He shoved Trent into the seats and braced himself.

The seraph came faster, dragging its massive form forward with bloodied limbs. It slammed into Seth with all its weight and he couldn't hold his ground. His back hit the emergency exit door hard, and the door itself popped out, ricochetting outward into the tracks. Seth managed to hold onto the seraph and kept himself from flying outside too.

But that wouldn't last long.

Hands from below the feathers shot out and gripped Seth's ankles, yanking his feet out from under him. With a shout, Seth hit the floor, half his body slipping out of the subway. His hands were still deep in the feathers, thankfully, keeping himself from slipping entirely.

With a guttural growl, the seraph gripped Seth's head with another hand and pushed him toward the tracks.

Shit, shit, shit! Trent had to do something. Seth couldn't hold on forever. Trent scrambled upright and charged the seraph. It barely registered his weight hitting it. He pulled at the feathers in fistfuls, yanking them out, but all that did was get him shot back to the seat with a bony arm.

"What did you do?!" the seraph screamed at Seth, a broken amalgamation of voices speaking at once. It shoved at Seth's face again, pushing him farther out of the subway. Sparks licked upwards from the tracks and Seth cried out in pain, slamming his palm against the seraph uselessly. "What did you do to us, you fucking nothing?!"

Trent forced himself back up, shaking his head to get his vision to stop swimming. He darted his gaze up and down the subway, searching for something to use.

There. One of the broken standing poles.

He dove for it, but the seraph didn't even look his way. He was an afterthought; the seraph's sole focus was Seth, pushing him into the tracks to be rid of him once and for all.

Trent brought the pole down as hard as he could on the seraph's back. It screeched, but didn't let Seth go. Trent hit it again and again, until the pole broke in two, but Trent kept on wailing anyway with the broken end. By then, he had the seraph's attention.

A pale hand shot out, latched onto Trent's throat, and yanked him off the floor. He kicked, swinging the half-pole, and the seraph twisted around to face him. The eye settled on him, enraged, bright like a bright bulb about to burst.

Until a gasp echoed from inside.

"The human!" a voice rasped.

"It's the human!" another one shouted at the same time, a mix of excitement and astonishment.

"The human! The human!" the voices crooned together, Seth all but forgotten as he lay half-conscious in the emergency exit doorway, his head lolling against the floor.

And now, Trent had no idea what to do.

"Be not afraid," came one voice, cutting through the others. It sent a shudder through Trent. The Leader.

Shit, he was still alive in there somehow. A sinister tenor dripped off his words. He didn't mean them. Not any longer. Probably never had.

Trent struggled harder, but it didn't matter what he did. He was caught.

The seraph slammed Trent into the floor. Trent's head bounced off the steel, making his vision spot white. The hands slammed him again, washing the pain over him anew. He wanted to throw up, it hurt so bad. He tried blinking back the white spots, clear his head, but then another slam came, ruining his efforts.

"I WANT HIS SKULL CRACKED OPEN!" the Leader screeched.

"Open! Open!"

"CRACK HIS RIBS OPEN!"

"To his heart, to his heart!"

"I WANT HIS HEART IN MY HANDS!"

Trent tried thrashing, but the seraph didn't

feel anything but rage. It slammed him down again. Blood bloomed in Trent's mouth. Deliriously, he realized he'd bitten his lip. A warm pain was spiderwebbing across the back of his scalp.

"This will work!" the seraph screamed, the voices as one. "It will! I will have his life!"

A flash of steel came down on the seraph's back, bright eyes glittering in the dark behind it. The seraph shrieked, swinging itself to the side, and Seth brought the pole down again with none of Trent's human hesitation. The neon halo cracked, shattered, and the pole made contact with a body. Blood flew. Splattered across the ceiling, the floor, and everything else in reach. When the seraph still maintained its hold on Trent, Seth gripped a wing and tore. The seraph screamed. Seth threw it aside, ignoring how it still twitched as it went.

Finally, the seraph let Trent go, leaving him crumpled on the floor, and swung an arm wide. Seth ducked low and shoved the pole upward into the seraph, like it was a sword. Right through the eye.

The ensuing scream was louder than the first and shook the subway. The air became bright, an oscillation visible as the sound attempted to tear the place in two. A large hand slammed into Seth, but he gripped another wing. It went with him, tearing right off the seraph. With another screech, the seraph spun all the way around. Blood sprayed with the spin, spewing across the subway car.

Trent propped himself up, trying to use the seat behind him as leverage. He was nauseous from the pain. Blood gushed from his mouth. But he had to see what was going on. He couldn't just lay there and let the dark have him.

Broken and bleeding, the seraph charged Seth again, but the maybe-angel was ready. He let the seraph come and tipped himself backward at the last second, toward the emergency exit. The seraph's momentum took it right over Seth and it flipped overhead with only one place to go: out the door and into the tracks.

Electricity tore into the seraph when it landed, bright blue unforgiving sparks overtaking its body. The horror screamed, its insides burning brighter and brighter, until its body popped. Blood and viscera coated the tunnel from the tracks, to the walls—everything—and then, it was gone around the bend.

Trent's strength left him. The subway jostled and Trent fell from the seat. The pain was so bad. The edges of his vision darkened quickly as he hit the floor again. He heard the gasp of his name. Felt hands gather him off the floor to lay his head on a lap. He blinked and found Seth staring down at him, bright eyes wide and worried. Seth's lap was comfy. The delirious thought stuck out in Trent's head, rising above the static of pain. He could stay here a while. He wouldn't mind.

The gentle touch of Seth's fingers through his hair jolted Trent back to himself. That motion also felt nice, something to fall asleep to, at least until Seth's fingers found their way to the back. Where the pain radiated. Trent gritted his teeth, and Seth quickly brought his hand back.

It was red. *Oh.* That was blood. Trent blinked hard. A lot of blood. *Shit.* Trent blinked again, trying to stay focused. Awake.

"No, no, no," Seth whispered. "Trent, stay with me, okay?"

"I'm fine," Trent slurred. He'd been hit harder before, hadn't he been, once upon a time? "This is nothing." Certainly didn't sound like nothing.

"You're bleeding." Seth used his shirt to wipe some of the blood off Trent's chin. The shirt blossomed with red, which was a shame. It was cute. "No, no, don't pass out on me. I can help. I can fix this. I know I can."

Trent blinked. Everything was so dark, Seth became a bright beacon anchoring Trent to consciousness. Even if he was blurry now. "Sure," Trent said, breathless. "Do what you gotta."

It was a moment before Trent's brain caught up to what Seth did once permission was given. Soft, warm lips encased his. Trent wouldn't have called it a kiss; it was too methodical. Too clinical. Whatever it was, the longer Seth remained there, the more Trent's head filled with the sound of what must have been divinity, right from the maybe-angel's mouth. He couldn't describe it any clearer than that. Even more, it reminded him of something. Pulled him toward it, letting reality—or whatever this really was—recede to it, allowing the pain to melt away. A memory once grown soft and blurry, now became bright beneath Seth's lips.

Verse Eight

A GLITTERING DREAM

The lights had been gauzy. An aftereffect of memory, maybe, but whenever Trent thought back to this moment, whenever he dreamed of it, that was how the lights were. A brightness fuzzed at the edges. Not quite real until Trent stood upon the stage, his guitar in hand, a riff singing into the air. It wasn't even a special night. One gig among the many in the same basement bar, just different bands, different decorations, different crowds.

The chords sung beneath his touch like always, its vibration carrying itself through the dancing bodies. Not that anyone was really listening; the music was a liminal backdrop to whatever was going on in their lives, nothing more. They wouldn't even remember it.

Then, among the lights, the colors, the bodies swaying with one another, a pair of eyes caught his. Brilliant glittering eyes, a dazzling kaleidoscope of colors reflecting the light. The only pair watching the band in earnest. Watching

Trent earnestly. Mesmerized and wide. Pretty.

The place was packed, one pair of eyes shouldn't have done what these did, but Trent couldn't look away. Like he was playing specifically for that pair of eyes. Like suddenly, his playing meant something to someone. A new fire lit in Trent's heart and he was sure that was the best he'd ever played.

Another band came on after his. He got paid. The rest of the band left because the scene really wasn't for them, but Trent stayed. Why had he stayed? He thought hard. Through the static eating away at the edges of the memory and pieced it back together.

The floor glittered with gold. Some New Year's decoration that had fallen too early. Trent was dancing with someone on top of it. His scuffed sneakers moved in time with a pair of bright red high tops. The glittering eyes that had watched him so intently, now holding his gaze so absolutely, it didn't matter who was brushing too close for comfort. Nothing could take Trent's attention away from these eyes. His name had been Seth, his mouth formed the words against Trent's ear when asked. Still barely heard above everything else, but Trent remembered it. Memorized it. And they danced and they danced amongst the glittering lights, their bodies pressed close together.

But the story hadn't ended there, Trent

reminded himself.

Their lips had found each other's beneath the gauzy lights. Lit up something in Trent's gut he couldn't douse. They stole away to the alley behind the bar, hands clasped as they led one another through the crowd. Snow had started falling by then, almost like crystalline glitter beneath the lamp outside. Trent pinned this Seth—not the one he knew now; this one with his bright hungry eyes and teasing smile—against the wall. Kept him there as their lips met again and again, chasing away winter's chill.

Kissing a stranger wasn't out of the ordinary; it was why Trent sometimes lingered after gigs. To find a genuine connection, or at least a mouth to get lost in for a little while before he had to find his way home, alcohol buzzing through his system. There was always another smile to kiss. To take for his own and to share his in return. Something to make him feel light, blissful, and happy, because that was why people did it right? To ignore their lives crumbling away beneath them, lost in someone else. When it was over and done with, Trent never remembered. Sometimes, he'd feel bad about it, but most of the time, it didn't matter. It wasn't like the smiles would remember him. Simply a shared, fleeting happiness.

This Seth, however, Trent had worked hard to memorize. How eager his mouth had been. How warm his delicate hands were as they ran themselves through Trent's hair. Under his shirt. He tasted like light. A drink to get lost in. They pulled at each other's clothes, eager to get them out of the way, but then Seth stilled. His back drew taut. A soft sigh like song escaped his soft lips and he pulled away from Trent.

He smiled and ran his knuckles across Trent's jaw. The light above made the colors dance inside his eyes. "I have to go," he whispered.

And like a fairy tale, he disappeared. A memory leaving Trent starkly alone in the alley, the taste of searing heat lingering on his lips. Trent had gone home, convinced it'd been a dream. One overexposed like a photo, its details washed out, as he tried to recall it every night.

But it wasn't a dream, Trent told himself, blearily coming awake.

He opened his eyes. The subway rocked back and forth, a familiar shift almost lulling him right back to sleep. Air gusted inside from the emergency exit, smelling like steel. The fluorescents above them were still blown, but it wasn't dark. Lights zipped by outside, blurs of orange creating a staccato of brightness as they passed. Blood left trails down the walls, making the whole car look like a horror film.

Trent was still on the floor, his legs folded underneath him, but his head had been laid on a seat that hadn't been covered in blood. The once blooming headache threatening to overtake everything was faraway now. Practically gone. A mere echo at best.

He blinked and noticed Seth this time, the maybe-angel—*his* maybe-angel—sitting so close, their knees were touching. Seth had his head on the seat too, close enough that his soft breaths brushed against Trent's face.

Trent was alive, at least. Had to count for something. Especially now because he was staring at the pair of brilliant glittering eyes he used to know.

Seth's face brightened with a hopeful smile.

"Are you with me?" he asked.

Trent swallowed; his throat was dry. "Yeah," he said. "What did you do?"

"Divine magic," Seth said. "It usually works via whispering, but it's much faster if I push the words *into* you. It stopped the bleeding."

Trent hummed. Words played in his head, each softly spoken by Seth himself, but they were too fragile to hold for long. As soft as a song misremembered. He gazed over Seth. Blood was all over him again. "So much for all that washing," he teased. "Covered in blood again."

Seth laughed, the sound delightful. "I know."

"Seth..." Trent whispered, desperate, and the maybe-angel paused, eyes flicking back to Trent's. "That Seth I knew..." Trent grabbed at the thought before it fled. Before he had to pay attention to anything else and it faded into memory once more. "It was you, wasn't it?"

Hesitating, Seth glanced away. "To be honest, I'd forgotten I'd told you that name," he whispered, twisting his hands in his lap. "When you said it then, when you called me by that name, cementing it as mine..." He closed his eyes with a soft sigh and shook his head. "Back then, seeing you, listening to you, giving myself a name—something I've never truly had before—changed a fundamental piece of me. It's not like I hadn't used fake names before. But that one? It felt like mine after you said it. I don't know why it happened then. Why seeing you there, hearing you play, did something to me. I don't know how to replicate it, but it made me... Well, *me*."

No longer a shadow like the other maybes. No more transitory food for seraphs to use as they would. Seth had made himself real by complete accident. Trent was impressed.

Seth opened his eyes, his expression soft.

"Even now, hearing you say my name... Something in my chest flutters knowing that it's *mine*. It remade me anew." Seth tilted his head, glancing away. "We're not supposed to be real like this. All I can think of sometimes is the pain it brings me when the seraphs find me and think I have an experience for them. I'm supposed to just... Stop. Disappear. Melt into them. Not linger like this, remembering the pain."

"Seth..." Trent whispered.

"Don't be sorry," Seth interrupted. "I love my name. I love being me. It's my life. Something small I made myself. They can no longer unmake me. I'll endure the pain, because past it, is the joy of being alive."

Trent hadn't thought of it like that. He smiled, relaxing against the seat again. "It was a random chance meeting," he said. "It never left me either, you know. Even after you disappeared, I thought of you a lot. Even as it grew soft."

"I wish I could have stayed," Seth said. "I barely had time for a goodbye."

"You could have told me you were him."

Seth snorted. "You swung a *mop* at me. I worried about forcing a connection when you hadn't yet made it yourself."

Good point. Had Seth opened with who he actually was, Trent might not have believed him, given the panicked state he was in. He shrugged, the motion reminding him that yes, he had a very achy body attached to his heavy head. His skin was tingling now, piecing feeling back together as it slowly awoke.

"This why you want to see my insides so bad?" Trent joked. "Think I have some truth buried in there somewhere?"

The laugh from Seth was soft, if a little embarrassed. "*Yes.* I want to know what it was about you that made something real inside me. Except I fully know that's not possible. There's more to it, but it's hard for me to explain what I really want. I don't even know."

"You don't have to." Trent tested his hands, flexing his fingers, as Seth grew thoughtful anyway. When all fingers were accounted for, Trent continued. "I bet I have some old x-rays or something. I can show you those. Kinda counts."

Seth blinked, eyes widening. "Do humans normally collect those?"

The curiosity was so cute and endearing, Trent couldn't help but grin. "Nah, I wanted to try making a bone record, but that was as far as I got." He'd needed much more equipment than he'd realized and only managed to get a hold of his old x-rays before giving up on the project.

Seth watched him, not quite understanding, and Trent bit back another laugh.

"It's uh... A way people back in the day smuggled banned music. The x-rays became the records. Sound quality was shit, apparently."

"Oh. Fascinating." Seth tilted his head. "I'd like to see one."

"Shit, me too. I always get outbid whenever one shows up online."

Seth snickered, ducking his head to hide the smile. The quiet laughter only lasted a moment before it trailed off. When Seth looked back up at Trent, he'd grown serious again.

"I listened for you, you know, when I couldn't die," he whispered, like if he spoke it too loudly, he'd be admonished. "I wanted to hear you again so, so badly. Whenever you practiced your guitar, I'd find it. Sometimes, I'd even hear you humming. I wanted to know all of your songs by heart. Just in case I saw you again."

Maybe all this time, Trent had never been alone. He hummed out one of the many melodies he'd penned. One he'd practiced in private until his fingers bled. One no one was supposed to know. Seth perked up and hummed with him. The same soft pitch, the same notes, never once missing a beat. Just hearing it so touched Trent deeper than he ever thought it would.

"That band kicked me out, you know," Trent admitted, honesty bubbling forth, and Seth frowned. "We clashed too much. Said I was a deadbeat. Not worth playing with. I dragged them down by not having my shit together."

It'd hurt at the time and the wound was still fresh. Trent knew that he wasn't blameless in the breakup; it'd become so easy to drink away negative thoughts. Easiest way to make himself forget a bad night. But then he lashed out. Then there were arguments because Trent was getting himself banned from venue after venue, severely limiting where they could play. He couldn't even remember half the shit he'd done. It was all stupid and frivolous; he wished he could take it back. Do some of those months over.

Trent choked on the words, the desire to be

honest and throw it all out there tangling itself in his throat, but he hardly got a few more stammered words in before Seth was reaching forward. He traced a hand gently through Trent's hair, pushing it back.

"I still enjoy listening to you," he said. "Band or no. I wish I'd been there to listen to you always."

"Can you?"

Maybe it was bold asking so. One night of bonding over the hell the seraphs were putting them through didn't mean anything.

"I... I don't know," Seth whispered. "I'm so used to borrowed flesh that is eventually ripped away from me, I've long since stopped dreaming I could stay in your world."

"But what about now?" Trent pressed on, taking Seth's hand in his. "They can't get rid of you now. You're real. You just need a way out. Come with me."

Seth looked taken aback, like he'd never considered it before. He stammered over his next words, shaking his head. "I-I... Is it silly to say I'm scared of trying? I'm still tenuously connected to the seraphs. What if one day they drag me back? I don't know if I can take it. Knowing I'm doomed, no matter what."

"Sometimes, it's worth trying, even if you're scared," Trent whispered. "I'll be there. I promise. I'll show you my x-rays. My guitar—I'll even teach you how to play it. And I'll introduce you to my cat.

She'll love you. Her name's Scotty. She's this stupid orange thing and will drool on you if you brush her because she loves it so much."

Trent was full on rambling, but he didn't care. He didn't want to be alone. Not after this. He didn't want Seth to be alone, either. Even if they were just friends, something more or something less, Trent wouldn't complain. It'd help having Seth there. The world would make a little more sense. Maybe not entirely right, but a step they could take together to enjoy living.

No answer came. Seth was glancing away again, suddenly shy, and Trent left it there. Didn't do any good to force Seth to say yes now when he was still unsure.

Letting Seth's hand go, Trent sat himself upright, groaning with the exertion. Pain from sitting too long radiated through his neck and knees. He was too old for this shit. Felt like he'd been on the wrong side of a mosh pit.

He turned himself, gritting his teeth, and pressed his back to the seat to stretch out his legs. Seth followed suit, sliding closer as he did so. He was warm, pressed against Trent's arm, and he rested his head against Trent's shoulder.

They watched the lights outside pass and pass. An orange streak cut across the inside before it was gone and then another one was chasing after it. Trent followed an orange streak across once and it illuminated the two seraph wings twitching on the seat across from them. Blood oozed around the stumps, staining the seats below. He cringed and Seth looked over.

"Ah." Seth nodded with a soft hum from his lips. "About those... I've a request."

Trent regarded Seth, suspicious. "Yeah? Does it involve me?"

"It requires a delicate hand."

Verse Nine

A DELICATE HAND

"I can't believe I'm doing this," Trent grumbled, the thread of light and heat pressed tight in his fingertips.

Seth wiggled teasingly until Trent tightened his legs around him. "I usually have a well-formed maybe help me sew my wings back on, but you're here. I trust you. Word of what we did to that seraph is probably spreading. Maybes are going to stay clear. Reinforcements are going to be looking for us soon, too, if they aren't already."

"What about the archangel you mentioned?"

Seth closed his eyes and pressed his ear to the subway floor. Trent wasn't sure how Seth was going to hear anything beyond the tracks below, but the maybe-angel must have. He frowned, eyebrows furrowing in worry.

"The hymn's almost finished. I still can't tell where he's being called, however."

Great. Trent wasn't looking forward to that.

"Having these wings will ensure I have more

power to face whatever is waiting for us once we emerge," Seth continued.

A sound plan, even if it meant Trent was doing something he'd never thought he would: sewing wings on an angel with a thread of pure light. This night just kept on getting weirder.

Seth didn't really explain what the thread was, except it was made from divine magic drawn from his voice. He'd sung ethereal words and out it came from his throat. The thread felt so delicate, Trent feared breaking it.

The skin where the other wings had been was raw and pink, but had healed enough to move the gauze out of the way. Seth told Trent to sew the new wings a little above the previous scars (and Trent tried not to count just how many there were crisscrossing where the wings had been).

Steeling himself with another swig from his water bottle, Trent steadied his hands. He took the light, its unseen needle, and pushed them into Seth's skin. Trent watched Seth's expression, ready to stop at any sign of pain, but Seth was pretty relaxed, his eyes closed in a serene expression.

"You good?" Trent asked anyway.

"Yes," Seth said, annoyed. "Just do it like I explained. You cannot hurt me." He smiled coyly, chuckling, and peered at Trent over his shoulder. "Besides, this is rather exhilarating."

Laughing, Trent shook his head to hide the warmth rushing his cheeks. He looped the thread into the twitching seraph wing and tried not to shudder that it still moved at all. He didn't want to know why. They'd found the subway's first aid kit earlier and used all the alcohol wipes within to clean the wings and the blood off their skin. Trent was looking forward to the long, hot shower awaiting him at home.

Trent pushed the thread through the wing's stump and leaned to one side as the whole wing flinched, as though trying to escape.

To ignore that, because the fact the wing might have been in pain bothered Trent more than he wanted to admit, he kept talking. "Are you just happy I'm straddling your ass?"

Seth hummed, barely smothering a laugh. "Could be. You are rather alluring there..."

Before whatever Seth said went to Trent's head (or another direction), he quickly diverted the conversation's course. "Got a more well-thought-out plan beyond 'find a place of worship and running for it?'"

Sighing, Seth tapped his fingers on the floor. The subway still rocked, but Trent had become one with the movements. He hadn't realized how long the route was, but it felt like they'd been on it forever already. It never made any stops, but Trent was glad for that. No more surprise seraphs. Although, that didn't stop him from glancing off into the dark with an occasional spike of worry.

"These wings will bestow upon me some of

the seraph's powers so I can better protect us," Seth explained. "Power is stored in the wings, after all. It's why the seraphs make sure to rip mine away whenever they catch me with some."

"Can you open the world like seraphs could with them?"

"Not just anywhere, still. That requires all five pairs of wings working in tandem."

"Of course it does."

"If I had a Rolls-Royce to take you home in and a way to do it, I'd do it."

Imagining rolling up to the rundown apartment building Trent lived in while inside a Rolls-Royce made Trent smile. If only.

Compared to Seth's more delicate frame, the wings were heavy and large. The feathers were scraggly and brown as well, their care clearly an afterthought. Trent preferred the soft look of Seth's other wings.

Thankfully, the stumps didn't need a lot of stitching. A loop here, there, and there, and then the wings fastened themselves to Seth's back, like they were locking in. Seth bit back a gasp when the first one did so, and hunched his shoulders. Trent hesitated before gently massaging the space between Seth's shoulder blades. Seth lifted a hand and waved it dismissively.

"Continue on," he said. "This is fine."

"You sure?"

"I am enjoying this, believe it or not. It was

just sudden. Move on."

The second wing went on like the first, quicker now that Trent had less hesitation about fucking it up. The thread of light went in and out, in and out, looped around there and here, and the wing situated itself. The skin shuddered, accepting the stump as its own, and out from Seth came another heated gasp. For good measure, Trent rubbed the spot between the wings, hoping that helped make them settle, and slid off Seth's back to let him move.

The wings stretched wide, bringing forth a low moan from Seth's lips as they went. He collapsed suddenly, gasping again, and Trent caught him.

"Shit!" Trent rolled him over. The maybe-angel was shivering, eyes even brighter.

"It's so much power," Seth breathed, covering his mouth. "I didn't think it'd be this much from just two. I can see the magic they wove around this place. The thrum of it in the air." He lifted an arm and traced something unseen with his fingertips. "This *is* divine."

It was another moment before Seth got a hold of himself. Trent helped him sit up, shaking his head. "Yeah well, you still look like shit."

Seth paused, indignant, and laughed, pushing Trent.

"Yes, I am fully aware of that." Seth tugged the straps of his tank top back across his shoulders.

"You do not look any better."

They shared a laugh, nudging each other back and forth. When it ebbed, Trent cleared his throat.

"Did I do a good job with the wings?" Trent asked, genuinely worried.

With a coy smile, Seth cupped Trent's chin with one hand and brought him closer. "Yes, you did. I'm sure you are hoping for a reward in the form of another kiss? A real one this time?"

To be truthful, Trent hadn't been angling for one, but he wasn't going to say no. Especially now that he knew this Seth was the one he'd met before. That they'd lived through murdering seraphs and took one down, even. A victory kiss would give Trent, maybe even Seth, some piece of happiness before everything went back to shit. Who knew what awaited them at the end of the line. Who knew if Trent would even get out.

Seth took Trent's shy smile as affirmation, and leaned forward slowly.

This one felt like an actual kiss. Soft and warm, their mouths fit together like they were made to. Divine words played on Seth's tongue, the sensation bright and loud, but they stayed there, teasingly out of reach. It made Trent chase them anyway, pushing their kisses deeper. This reminded him of the kiss from the alley. The fervent desire spilling over, lost in each other like it would be their last. Trent wanted to lay Seth back down, pull him open just like Seth had wanted to do to him, but the worry of pushing things too far stopped Trent. As though in response to the sudden longing, the divine words on Seth's tongue pressed against Trent's. They became electric in all the right ways, sending pleasure right through Trent's body. He never wanted to let go of that feeling. He wanted it to trace him from the inside out, to make a home for itself in him, until he was the one teasing Seth with divine words he'd taken as his own. They could chase each other's divinity until one of them lost their breath. Until their lips slipped. Until their lungs burned too much for air. But Trent never wanted to let go; he wanted to be here until he couldn't, lost within Seth.

An announcement droned over the subway, bringing Trent back to reality. A stop approached.

Seth drew back, a satisfied smirk on his lips despite his own breathlessness. He drummed his fingers on Trent's chin teasingly. "Back to reality," he said.

If only they could have stayed there for longer, drowned in each other until nothing at all mattered but themselves.

"Back to reality," Trent agreed and helped Seth to his feet.

The subway brakes hissed softly, coming to a halt, and the doors opened. With a deep breath, Seth led the way. He'd left his jacket behind, folded neatly on the seat as though he might come back to it. Part of Trent hoped he could; it looked cute on Seth.

For now, Seth's new seraph wings elegantly tucked around his midsection as though to give him warmth. Trent followed closely behind him.

Though Trent expected an immediate assault from the seraphs, nothing was there to greet them. The subway platform was a ghost town. Not even a busker's song. What Trent hated, however, was that the stop was familiar and not at the same time. He should have known it, he sort of did—the lingering graffiti, the layout, where the exit was just up the steps—but it felt wrong. He'd never seen it so empty and deserted, even late at night. The pillars once graced with fliers of all kinds were filled with graffiti of eyeballs and wings. The ticket counters were dark and empty, like no one had ever sat behind them. None of the digital interfaces on the turnstiles were lit up. Everything was in its correct place, but hollow. Like an echo of reality.

"Why does it always look like this?" Trent finally asked, the silence banging up his nerves. "Like my world, but deader somehow?"

"Because it *is* dead." Seth slipped over the turnstile with ease, a practiced motion. Trent followed him over. "It's an echo that was never meant to be alive because seraphs have no idea what that means. They take broad strokes and paint them haphazardly to pretend. Even with all the cracks and rust, this is enough for them."

The walls were all crumbled and rotted through as they made their way out. The only thing beyond was a network of fences, keeping an omnipresent darkness contained. At the entrance, the front windows had cracks spiderwebbing from floor to ceiling, and one window was bashed through entirely. Shards lay on both sides. Around the doors were once displays for advertisements, but they had been burned through like an electrical fire had sparked. Scattered newspaper and trash littered the ground around the doors, blown in by a cold wind. Seth stepped over the mess without a second glance.

The stop was up on a hill and looked down at the city before it. When Trent was younger, he'd sit up on this hill and watch the city streets in the dead of night when he didn't want to go home. He still did that, sometimes.

Back then, the streetlights made a vibrant line all the way down. Late night traffic would become the stars he counted. Everything glittered then as something bright to stare at until his eyes watered. He missed it.

Especially now because it was no such thing.

A yawning darkness covered the streets, making it blend into the dark sky above. Buildings were darker shapes and any light they did have, was a bright red window like before. The still-standing streetlights flickered every so often, splitting the darkness for a second, but not for long enough to see well. What cars lined the road were dead, lights completely absent. It was like gazing at the end of the world.

Past the burned-out traffic lights and darkness, at the bottom of the hill, was light. The church. It didn't look at all like the one Trent knew. This was a jagged spire of pristine white stone, cutting through the dark around and above it. Immaculate while everything else around it rotted. A golden halo rotated around the tip if its spire, forever turning.

Trent's gaze was pulled past the halo. Farther upward, following what was *attached* to the tip of the spire. A red, translucent ribbon, leading to a pulsing red membrane suspended in the sky, the lights within beating in time with a heartbeat.

The longer Trent stared at it, the more his head hurt. The more the view tore at the edges. He squinted his eyes, trying to get a better look. There was the shadow of something within. One magnified by the crown of light haloing it, like the very being within was holy.

What it could be hit Trent like a brick. He gasped.

"That's God," Seth said. He was coming back from a pile of rubbish, a new lead pipe over his shoulder. "Don't stare at Him. The view will burn out your corneas before long."

Trent snapped an alarmed look at Seth.

"Right above my city? *That's* where God is?"

"He's everywhere," Seth corrected. "This is but one vision of Him. He is omnipotent, omnipresent and appears around places of worship. Waiting. Listening to the creation He gave life to. And with Him are always angels."

"And down there is the only way out?" Trent asked, panic already pushing his pulse into his ears. "Go near the thing they want my blood for?"

Seth peered up at him, smiling crookedly. "Looks that way," he said.

Eyes opened up around God, making Trent jump. They were bright cuts through the sky, almost like searchlights, but then they closed in the same breath. The silhouettes of seraphs flitted through the sky, lit up whenever the eyes opened. Maybe other angels were with them too. A holy song jaggedly put together echoed across the sky, a kind of demented lullaby.

"All right." Trent steeled himself with a deep breath. A second one because the first failed to do anything. All the panic rolling back through his body couldn't stop him. He wasn't ever brave; it was easier not to be. Although right now, he had to be. Maybe he'd change. Maybe this was what it took to jumpstart a life he felt like living. "All right."

"It's okay to be afraid." Seth slid his hand along Trent's until Trent opened his so Seth could hold it. "Were you ever scared standing on the stage?"

"No," Trent said, incredulous at the thought. "I looked past people. Focused on the music in my head. It was just me and my guitar." Too bad he didn't have it now. Wouldn't have been any help, it'd probably get broken, but its weight would have been familiar. Grounding. Like a security blanket. It would have meant things were normal.

Taking another deep breath, because his guitar wasn't there, Trent swallowed the cold air that tasted like fire. He exhaled it slowly, trying to remember how. After a few more of the same motions, he squeezed Seth's hand.

"After this, you should come to my side," he said softly. "I hum better in person."

A genuine smile crossed Seth's lips. "If I have someone to hold my hand, maybe I can."

"I can be that person," Trent said. "If you want me to be. We can wake up early and watch dawn together." He gently nudged Seth. "So long as your demon doesn't mind."

Seth chuckled. "He's not the hand-holding type. I'd love it if it was you."

They shared a smile. Trent wanted to kiss Seth's smile, just to make them both feel more emboldened because that was what you did, right? But he left the moment as it was. A kiss could come later. When they both lived past this moment. When they found each other once again on the other side because Trent had to believe they would.

Together, they stared at the spire of worship.

"So?" Trent asked. "If we run, they'll get us."

Seth hummed in agreement. "Yes, I see that. There's more than even I had anticipated." He gazed down the street and stopped. A wicked smile slid across his lips. He tugged eagerly on Trent's hand.

There was a vintage looking car a jog down the road. Seth nodded at it. "How do you feel about convertibles?"

Verse Ten

BURNING HALO

Honestly, Trent was surprised he could hotwire the convertible. That he'd even remembered how. A useless skill he'd learned as a kid quickly made obsolete by modern cars now suddenly useful. Even more surprising: the convertible had gas and a radio that worked.

"Seraphs like their cars," Seth said, like it explained anything. Trent accepted it anyway and fiddled with the radio to find *something* to listen to.

As the radio's speakers gave bursts of static from turning the dial, Seth settled himself in the passenger seat and checked the compartments within reach. Nothing useful. Sighing, Seth climbed up to the top of the seat and braced himself there with his legs, ready with the lead pipe.

Trent hoped to find rock music of some kind, but most of the stations spewed static except for one. Classical. So be it. Tchaikovsky's 1812 Overture it was. As the notes washed over him,

Trent steeled himself in the driver's seat. Talked himself up in his head, that he'd survive, that Seth would survive, and was still doing so when Seth bent close and kissed his cheek. The warmth was soothing and practically melted through Trent.

"For luck," he said.

Nodding, Trent looked out onto the street again. He hesitated. There had to be something he could do. Something he could give Seth in return to share some of the luck. He pulled out the chain holding his guitar pick. It must have gotten him this far, surely. Maybe it would keep Seth safe once everything was over and done with.

Seth watched him curiously as Trent beckoned him to dip his head forward. The maybe-angel did so without asking why and Trent looped the necklace around Seth's neck.

"For luck," Trent said, kissing the guitar pick before he let it go. "Whatever happens, I expect you to give that back to me someday."

Smiling softly, Seth touched the guitar pick and admired the sunflower on it. He nodded. "I will. Are you ready? I think we've one shot at this."

"I'm ready." Trent revved the engine. "You better hold on tight."

He reversed, lined the convertible up with the center of the road, and switched gears. The engine rumbled, singing through the air. Trent breathed out and punched it. The convertible flew almost, wheels coming down on the pavement hard as they cleared the crest of the hill, and Trent pushed the pedal to the floor.

The roar of the engine heralded their entrance for all those in the sky listening. A misaligned chorus was the answer, raising up from the darkness, and chased after them. Screeches of *"be not afraid"* rang out from all sides as feathers shot toward them, just missing the convertible. Unmerged seraphs dove toward them, some slamming into the ground with crunches of blood and bone that punctuated the music, and others swooped to attack Seth, who stood unwavering with his lead pipe poised.

Except it was no longer a lead pipe; light had enveloped it, morphing it into a glowing sword. A different hymn, one more divine, echoed off the blade like it really was a holy weapon, and the sound became louder every time it burned seraphs through. Even with the new weapon, however, it became apparent too soon that Seth's only failing was that he was one person with one sword.

He swung one seraph out of the way, but then another collided into him before Trent could warn him, and Seth and the seraph were thrown into the backseat.

Shit! Another seraph was coming at Trent with a frontal assault. Trent swerved, narrowly missing it, and swung the wheel back the other direction to get back on track.

He forgot to look above him. A seraph landed

on the hood of the convertible, jostling the car, and held on long enough to stand.

"Be not afraid," it crooned, blood gushing down its mouth.

"Fuck you!" Trent slammed on the brakes. The sudden force, the inevitable spin as Trent swung the wheel around, flung the seraph off. As he straightened the car, a screech from behind made him jump. The previous seraph went flailing out of the back, its wings on fire.

Seth climbed back to the front, taking deep breaths. He bisected another seraph coming their way and flung it off the blade into another one. Both burned on impact, making a crater in the ground. More and more descended from the sky in a fury, screeching and clawing at Seth, like they intended to carry him off if they could just get a good grasp on the maybe-angel.

It was a struggle, wings flapping and flailing, but by then, they were close enough to the spire. Trent slammed the brakes again and turned the wheel. The spin threw the seraphs off balance, right out of the car, and sent Seth into Trent's lap. The car slammed sideways against the church, bouncing off it before coming to a stop, and Trent and Seth looked out at their wake.

Seraphs were forcing themselves to their feet, limbs bent at broken angles, wings crooked and skeletal from all the feathers the sword had burned away. Some of them were coming together as one, cannibalizing the more broken ones until they became a single mass, another horror. More monstrosities came down from the sky, shaking the ground as they landed.

Seth jumped out of the car and slid across the hood. Trent went after him. Just as he cleared it and ducked on the other side, the seraphs descended on the convertible.

"Help me open the door!" Seth shouted.

Trent hopped back to his feet, seeing Seth struggling with the massive church door, and threw himself at it. With both of them, they threw the doors open at the same time. As the seraphs regrouped behind them, screaming, Trent and Seth dragged each other through and slammed the doors shut.

They were inside.

Trent intended to stay standing, brace the doors while they got their bearings, but his legs were jelly. They folded underneath him almost immediately. Seth caught him, but Trent was too heavy for Seth to keep upright. They both sprawled to the floor, on top of one another.

Seth began laughing first, trying to bury the sound in Trent's shoulder, but it was so infectious, Trent couldn't help but join in. They were inside. Safe. Just one more thing and he'd be home. Out of this hell, hopefully with Seth by his side.

As they got a hold of themselves, the laughter tapering off to a soft echo bouncing through the room, Trent took in the church around them.

It was deceptively small. A single round room of white stone reaching high. Stained-glass windows went around and above, each one a picturesque painting of an angel. What the seraphs might have been before all this. Pillars went around the center of the room, reaching high as well. Beams were attached to the pillars and from them hung vibrantly colored drapery, ready to enclose the center of the room at a moment's notice.

"Now what?" Trent asked, breathless.

"Now—"

A sudden brightness stole the words away, creating a tear in the air in the center of the room. Trent looked up, eyes wide, and Seth swore. Trent had no time to figure out what he was looking at before the air lifted Trent and Seth off the floor and slammed them into the doors.

"Shit!" Trent cried. The brightness was growing, shaping itself. "What the fuck is that?" he forced out through gritted teeth. He couldn't move.

"The archangel," Seth breathed. His eyes were shut tight. "Of course, this was where they were summoning him—I should have known."

The light finished convalescing and Trent and Seth were dropped to the floor. The pain zinged itself up Trent's body as he landed, but he caught himself from being laid flat. Seth jumped to his feet first, collecting his light sword from the floor, and readied himself to strike.

In the center, a man appeared. He was rising from a crouch, a circle of symbols glowing like embers around him. He was tall with detail befitting a marble statue cracked with gold. Flowing golden hair frozen in time spilled behind him, the strands decorated with brilliant pearls. A pair of wings unfurled wide, each a pure white that shined all on its own. As he straightened his back, a halo of golden fire drew itself around his head. He hurt to look at directly. Trent's eyes watered just trying.

The archangel turned and the brightness was turned up tenfold. It pushed its way through the entire room, eating away all shadow until everything inside was laid bare in stark light. The angel opened his eyes wide, a molten gold with white irises, and looked right at them.

A sword materialized like a shot in the archangel's hands. At first, just a white blade, but then fire roped around it like a ribbon. He did not charge with it, however. He stood there, waiting. Watching.

The doors vibrated behind Trent. Fists pounded against it from the other side, trying to get in. The same sounds came from the stained-glass windows. The outline of hands pounded them just as hard, trying to get through. It made the whole room shake. Trent too.

"What do we do?" Trent whispered.

"Look behind the archangel," Seth replied.

An altar of marble and gold stood in the center of the room behind the archangel, and a white basin sat at the top. Inside looked to be water, glistening a million different colors.

"That's the holy water we need. It's made from manifested prayers," Seth continued. "I can open a tear in our worlds with it, but it will only last a brief moment." Seth swallowed and his shoulders tensed. "The archangel knows this. That's why he's not moving. We have to get over there and spill it."

Trent looked at Seth, worried. "And you?"

The lack of an immediate answer made Trent want to rethink their plan, but Seth took his hand before he could.

"Won't be the first time I've had to piece myself together," Seth whispered. "I'm real. I'm alive. They won't take this from me." He looked up at Trent, eyes clear with conviction. "I will get you out of here alive."

The air shimmered around the archangel, and he cocked his head to one side, eyes sliding from Trent to Seth and then back.

"*This need not be difficult,*" the archangel crooned, but fuck if Trent knew what he'd actually said. The words came in snatches, echoes, and Trent's mind filled in the blanks. "*Give up and you will know forever peace.*"

"Fuck you!" Trent shouted.

The archangel narrowed his eyes, but he didn't move away from the altar. A stalwart guard. Although, Trent wasn't sure what he would have done if the angel *had* charged them then.

There had to be another way to goad the angel into moving, but as Trent tried, tears slid out of his eyes. Watching the archangel *hurt*. It was like staring at the sun. As Trent blinked away the bright spots tearing into his vision, Seth gently turned Trent's chin.

A much softer angel to look at. They held each other's gazes for a few heartbeats, even as it sounded like the whole building would come down around them.

"I'll handle the goading," Seth said. "Ready?"

"No choice, I guess?" Trent asked.

With a smile, Seth stood on his toes and kissed Trent. It was quick and soft, but the electric spark of divine words lingered anyway. A promise. Trent held onto it as he and Seth faced the archangel together. As one.

The stolen seraph wings unfurled wide behind Seth and he shot forward, yanking Trent with him.

With strength Trent hadn't realized Seth had, the maybe-angel whipped Trent forward. He screamed unbidden, sliding across the pristine floor on his ass, and went right underneath the archangel's legs. For a brief moment, the archangel took his eyes off Seth to face Trent, incredulous, but that gave Seth an opening. The maybe-angel went high with the lead pipe sword. The archangel's recovery was too quick, however; the fire sword came up in a flash and blocked the attack. That was all Trent could see before he hit the altar, knocking it over like they wanted.

Holy water doused him and the floor, tasting like nothing and everything at the same time when it hit his tongue. It quickly spread, like oil, coating the tiles in the shimmering liquid.

Seth's cry of pain pulled Trent back to the fight. A body thumped somewhere beyond the bright monstrosity. Trent scrambled on his hands and knees, vision spotted with white from fucking looking, and he grabbed the bowl. He chucked it as hard as he could at the archangel.

It smashed into the bright spot threatening to burn out Trent's eyes. He dove to one side, narrowly missing a sword of fire cleaving through the air toward him. The altar burned to ash and a mark seared itself into the wall behind it.

"*You will not escape,*" the archangel said, his voice soft, but there was a threat behind the words. "*He will wake and all will be free.*"

Shit, shit, shit! Trent scrambled backwards, slipping on the holy water to get away, but all of that had been the opening Seth needed. He came out from behind the curtains, rebounding off one of the pillars, eyes bright, wings wide, and impaled the pipe through the archangel's neck. The bright blade went all the way through, spilling white blood across the tiles.

The blood glowed as it hit the holy water, ghosting light into the air like little auroras.

But the archangel wasn't dead. Far from it. With an anguished cry that oscillated visible waves through the air, shattering the windows, the archangel turned on Seth. Before the maybe-angel could disengage, one hand latched onto a wing. Between Seth pushing himself away and the archangel tearing his hand backward, the wing tore from Seth's back.

Blood sprayed over the archangel, staining his marble façade red, but Seth didn't let the pain stop him. He used the momentum of being free of the wing to twist around the archangel's form. With a spin, the archangel followed him, but he wasn't fast enough before Seth threw his entire weight at the angel. The turn had left the archangel unsteady and the sudden weight made his knees buckle, sending him and Seth crashing to the floor.

All was still for a single moment. Then the air warmed, like fire streaked across it. Embers licked into view, rising high, and Seth threw himself at Trent. Their bodies collided, sliding across the holy water, and they dodged the sword of fire coming down for them. The hulking mass of light was getting up. Seraphs were trying to climb in through the shattered windows, a chorus of their voices screeching as glass tore into their arms and wings.

But Trent focused on Seth. The soft hymns exhaling from his lips as he dipped his finger into the holy water. The surface undulated softly, ripples first becoming colors and then vibrant lights as it moved away from them. As quickly as he could, Seth drew a circle around Trent.

And then Trent dipped. Knees and hands went into the floor. An ice-cold sensation gripped him and held him there. He balked and looked at Seth. The maybe-angel met his gaze, his face freckled in blood, both white and red, and he smiled sadly. He wasn't sinking with Trent. Their held gaze lasted a single moment. A held breath. A heartbeat shared between them. All before the world kickstarted back into motion.

Seth swung himself to the side, the sword slice narrowly missing him as it singed the air, and the ground swallowed Trent up. He couldn't resist the pull of the dark liquid below him. As he sank, struggling against what felt like water, just to reach up to drag Seth with him, seraphs descended into the spire. Their chorus was muted and distorted by the water's ripples and he sank further still, searching for Seth in the scatter of wings and feathers above him. The seraphs went after someone, screaming, but the blur of white with a single dark wing was too fast. The perfect distraction. Trent would have cheered if he knew Seth would have heard him.

The desire lasted until the archangel blocked the view. He appeared so suddenly, Trent flinched. The angel's form was a bright eclipse, encompassing everything. From the angel came a gulf of hatred attempting to drown Trent, but Trent wasn't afraid. He stared back, defiant.

The archangel reached in, grasping for Trent, but it was too late. Trent had sunk too far into the dark. The marble white hand ribboned apart, the dark tearing into it, and the archangel immediately retracted his hand. He couldn't come in. Whatever this world was in the dark pool, wasn't for archangels.

Trent laughed, unable to hold it in, and threw up two middle fingers for the archangel. A shriek pushed through the water, but it never reached Trent. He was too far gone.

Trent sank faster and faster, until the brightness above was but a pinprick, leaving him in total darkness. But by then, the world was melting into a milky white below him, like he'd gone from one place to the next. Trent fell into the new light, the warm haze accepting him as he was. It was almost like a fuzzy dream bleeding past him. Bright and brilliant, like Seth's eyes.

Like Seth's eyes underneath gauzy lights...

Trent jolted upright, half a snore frightening him out of his doze. Everyone stared. Those on the pews in front of him and even the judgmental fucks beside him. Not his fault they'd sat here in the very back with him. Nothing about him said he was as pious as they were, so they could go fuck right off.

He blinked, cutting off his own glare, and glanced forward. He was in a *church*. In the middle of a *service*.

The wrongness hit him at once. He'd never been in a church before in his *life*. He let that settle in his head, trying to piece together why he was even here. The pastor droned on, unaware of the stare down going on in the back. He was describing something about fear. Trent scoffed. What middle-aged white pastor knew anything about fear? Trent tuned him out, drawing his attention elsewhere.

Stained-glass windows surrounded the pulpit, each one a vibrant splash of abstract color. Sunlight shone through them, making the air shimmer. Except no, those didn't look right. Trent blinked. The afterimage of broken glass spilled across the pulpit. The sound echoed in his ears. Except those weren't the windows Trent had seen shattered from an anguished cry.

His heart thumped, trying to figure out what was the lie. He blinked again and pinched himself. He flinched immediately. His skin was raw, like it had come too close to a fire. It was then he realized, this wasn't his jacket.

Gasping, he braced himself on the pew in front of himself, ducking his head down low.

The angels. The seraphs. The glass. *Seth*. He stood suddenly, drawing more concerned eyes his way. The pastor continued on, still oblivious. Trent whispered an apology as he squeezed out of the pew to escape.

Everything hurt, from the back of his head to the tips of his toes, but this was *his* reality. He was home, but Seth wasn't with him.

The receptionist gave him a pity look when he asked where the restroom was, but she helpfully pointed him in the right direction. No one was in there. Good.

The tiles were immaculate, clearly cleaned daily. They were immediately scuffed as Trent shuffled through, ash left in his wake. Bright sunshine shone through a frosted window at the far end, lighting the place in soft shades of morning, at odds with Trent himself.

He braced himself on the sink and stared at his reflection. God, he really looked like he'd just escaped Hell. Dark circles rimmed his eyes. The golden-brown stubble around his face was flecked with blood. His cheeks were smudged with what looked like ash. Aged ten years in a single night it felt like. Not to mention the dried blood all over his shirt and in his hair.

No wonder everyone was staring at him.

He bent over the sink and splashed water on his face. Scrubbed it through his hair until he felt clean. The water was ice cold. It soothed the phantom burns across his skin. He looked marginally more put together when he caught himself in the mirror again.

And he couldn't help it. He touched his face. Pinched it to be sure he was actually here.

"Seth?" he whispered at his reflection. "Seth, are you there?"

Nothing answered him. Only his reflection stared back. The mirror wasn't anything more than that. Had it been real? He squeezed his fingers around the edge of the sink until they hurt. It had to be real. He pulled open his jacket and looked for his guitar pick. It wasn't there.

Which meant Seth had to have it.

"Seth," he spoke, focusing on where Seth must have been on the other side. If it even existed there. "If you can hear me, I was serious. I'll be here. I'll hold your hand, just... Just come find me."

It was all he could do because he couldn't go back in there and find Seth on his own. Assuming the archangel hadn't ripped him in half. If he was even still Seth after all that.

No. Trent couldn't think like that. Seth *was* still himself. He'd escape the seraphs and the archangel and that was that.

The smile Seth had given him in the end fixed itself in Trent's mind. A bright memory. The soft lips. The way his eyes crinkled, bright and starry.

Without anything else to do or say, Trent left the church. Welcomed winter's cold sun on his face as he stepped outside, and lingered to *feel* it. It felt so good to see the blue in the sky. Not the omnipresent darkness lining every which way limned in red. This was real.

Then, he went home. More questions than answers bubbled at the edge of his thoughts, but he'd have to live with them. Instead, he focused on the lingering touch of Seth's mouth on his. The fervent prayer therein that they'd find each other again.

Verse Eleven

FERVENT PRAYER

After his return from Hell (because what else could it have been?), Trent moped for a few days, too afraid to leave his apartment. Scotty had been overjoyed at his return and happily followed him as he paced, sat with him as he tried to make sense of everything, and slept on his chest at night, purring up a storm. Nights left him paralyzed with the existential dread of what if this was the night some seraph grew smart enough to finish the job, but all Trent had to do was remind himself of the seraphs he'd fought. Survived. They'd *never* get over their shortsightedness. And besides, if they ever did, it wasn't like Trent would know.

Reminding himself of that gave him a little solace. Helped him move on from the nightmare. Seth was still out there, listening for him. Trent couldn't just hole himself up at home; he'd never find Seth that way.

In the daylight, Trent began humming to himself more. Especially if he was waiting for the subway or while he was in a restroom. Most of the time, it was only his voice, but sometimes, he heard a soft echo repeat his verses. A softness to the air, touching his skin. His lips.

Maybe it was in his head. A dying hope.

After the first few listless days, he revisited the church. He felt weird going inside, knowing that what it stood for was much more complicated than anyone would believe.

He stopped going once he convinced himself Seth wouldn't be waiting for him there. Not his speed, especially with all those seraphs. He'd be smart enough to be elsewhere.

As winter continued on, normalcy returned. Trent started going to gigs again; Patty's band had indeed been in need of a new guitarist and she happily let him play. Whenever he went out with them, he'd search the crowd for a pair of familiar, glittering eyes. He never found them, but he played like he did anyway, feeling a presence listening to him somewhere in an empty bar full of rusted walls, music thrumming through the thin boundary between their worlds.

It wasn't a dying hope. Trent had to believe that Seth was somewhere, listening still. He had to be. Thinking so got Trent through the more somber days.

As it grew warmer, leaves blossoming along the trees with spring flowers popping up all over the place, Trent began retracing his once path through the park. He was hoping for something familiar. Daring the world to try taking him again. He'd be ready this time for five angels in the parking lot.

Most of the time, he got through the park without meeting anyone.

Whenever he went, he made sure to hum. Beats of a new song he was writing or maybe an old one that Seth would know. He listened to the wind rustle in return, hoping an echo would give him the tune back.

It was 3AM again and he was passing the park once more on his way home. So close to the path he'd taken that night and he decided to hell with it and gave it another try. He had his guitar with him this time. Tonight, the restaurant had let him entertain a crowd of literally two people. It was weird, but the couple seemed to enjoy it; he'd gotten fantastic tips.

He was hoping to find a place to practice on the way home. Sometimes, the night made songs feel right. Or maybe Trent just wanted to sing to the stars. His fingers weren't freezing, at least.

The tunnel was still there and would probably always be there. Still pitch-black inside, too. With his new phone, Trent shined a light over the graffiti. The images of demons had been wiped clean; in its place were tagged slogans, caricatures of known cartoons doing crass things, and eyes all over the place telling the viewer someone was watching. Eerie. Below everything, he saw shades of what had been there before. Buried, but bleeding through. Much like his own memories.

With each day that passed, what happened softened like it really had been a dream. Every morning, Trent reminded himself of the horror he'd survived. That it was real and not just a fucked-up dream. He still had the jacket and the weird band t-shirt. More importantly, forcing himself to acknowledge the reality of the Hell he'd dragged himself through helped him remember Seth's face. He couldn't forget it. He'd almost done that once before and he was not going to let himself do it again. Seth was real and he *would* find a way out of there. He promised.

No one was waiting for Trent in the parking lot past the tunnel tonight. No angels. No Rolls-Royce. The light was bright, newly fixed. It was one of the new LEDs, an eye-searing blue instead of a soft orange. Trent missed the orange.

Still, it was as good a place as any to hunker down and practice for a bit. He settled on a chipped parking block and pulled out his guitar. This one wasn't the one he used at larger gigs. It was too sentimental for that, being his first serious guitar. Stickers decorated the body, most of them from old bars, bands he'd played with, and definitely mistakes. He'd added a recent one to the mix: a pair of pearlescent angel wings he'd bought from a vendor a few weeks ago. Seemed fitting.

The guitar sung softly into the stars, the universe, and maybe past that too. Trent hoped, at any rate. And if not, at least he was playing again. He'd missed this. Being in his head where it was only him and the music.

The longer he played, the more he hummed with it. The song didn't quite have its lyrics yet, but they were getting there.

Halfway into the song, the air shimmered in front of him. Tore. Burned at the edges. The light above Trent flickered. Trent's heart kicked up, beating hard, but he wasn't going to be afraid. He kept playing, growing bolder as he slid his fingers across the bridge. The air continued to shimmer in response, bright and brilliant, and it was almost too much. Trent didn't close his eyes, though, worried he'd miss something if he did.

Warmth touched him first. Soft, delicate fingertips traced his face. The brightness dimmed and died, letting him see. Glittering eyes met his. Ones he knew. Ones he dreamed of knowing again. Paired with the stardust freckles and the same coy smile.

Seth was bending over to be level with Trent and was drawing his fingers slowly through Trent's hair. Trent couldn't help but smile back. Relief washed through him at once.

"You made it," Trent said, hoping his voice didn't break the moment.

"Took some time, a few favors, finding where

the seraphs left the worlds thin... but yes." Seth smiled so warmly, Trent was sure something inside of himself melted. "I had to. I promised."

Seth hadn't changed. Fluffy white hair cut haphazardly paired with his brilliantly bright eyes. He was wearing his floral sleeved satin jacket off his shoulders, showing off his wing tattoos. A black tank top replaced the cute one with the deer. Distressed black skinny jeans hugged his legs tightly and were rolled up at the ankles to make room for his usual vibrant red high tops. The shoes were a little more singed along the soles, but still whole. The guitar pick necklace hung from his neck, its painted sunflower still bright.

He didn't have wings, though. The urge to know what favors and from who and how exactly Seth managed to slip through the worlds without the aid of wings bubbled through Trent's thoughts, but he let them go. Let the mystery hold for a little longer; Trent didn't want to ruin their reunion.

He leaned into Seth's hands, turning his head to kiss Seth's palm, and focused on how real and warm they felt.

"I missed you," he said.

"I missed you, too," Seth said. "Your hair's longer. I miss the scruffiness."

"Still think I'm cute?"

Seth tilted his head, making Trent come with him. The smile grew, making his eyes crinkle. "Yes, yes I do." He cupped Trent's face and gave him a kiss.

It lingered long enough to be teasing, but Trent didn't mind Seth cutting it short. Still lit a fuzzy feeling in his gut. Seth sat next to him on the parking block and pressed himself close.

"I listened for you, you know."

"Yeah?" Trent drew his fingers across the guitar strings, letting the riff sing into the air.

"Yeah." Seth wrapped his arms around Trent's and leaned further into him. "I want to listen more. I hope you aren't done playing."

"I can play all night if you want me to," Trent whispered. "All day, too."

With a soft, pleased sigh from his lips, Seth rested his head against Trent's shoulder. He looked so at peace there, like he'd never leave if Trent let him. Trent was okay with that. He leaned his head against Seth, smiling all the while.

Trent played into the night, the notes soft and sure. Seth hummed along, his voice a pleasant vibration against Trent's arm. Real. Not a dream. They sat there like that, their combined music singing into the air, all the way until dawn broke in earnest. Seth paused then, raising his gaze to the vibrancy of the sun coming through the trees.

He smiled widely, the glitter of dawn bright in his eyes.

Acknowledgments

I'm not going to lie, this idea came together like lightning and wrote just as fast. One day, I was listening to Kiki Rockwell's *Seven Angels Greet me in the Carpark* and failing to be good at playing a la mode games's *Sorry, We're Closed* (seriously, it's a good game, I just suck at it), and this idea wormed into my head. Add in a dash of Silent Hill because that's my go-to inspiration for *any* horror and out came Trent's very bad night feat. angels.

Every fever dream of an idea like this has someone who immediately gives eyes emoji upon hearing the basic premise (it's got angels in it and its horror). That is of course, Miranda, who likes horror angels about as much as I do.

Thank you also to my beta-readers who read this quickly and efficiently, helping me get it ready faster than I thought possible. Aowna, Jake, Royal, Emily, and Vincent, your thoughts on the story were incredibly helpful and the story wouldn't be what it is now without your help. And thank you to M. Rhys Bail for your valuable insight on editing and making the story cooler.

And of course, thank you to my mom for cheering me on no matter the project.

About the author

S. Jean (they/she) is a queer sci-fi & fantasy author writing whatever strikes their fancy at any given moment. When not writing or dreaming of what to write, they can be found dabbling in game dev and drawing!

For more information,
visit: https://sjean.carrd.co/